"Tyler, turn me loose," Lacey ordered.

"Nope," he said, moving his mouth toward hers.

Not again, she begged silently. Too late. She was being kissed, thoroughly kissed, and there was no way to stop him. Tyler finally drew back and grinned down at her with undisguised joy.

"Tyler," she protested, "you don't know what you're doing."

"You're right, and it's been a long time since ignorance felt so good. Kiss me, Lacey."

"I won't," she said. The act of refusing died a quick death as his mouth captured hers again. His fingertips teased beneath her blouse and tickled the delicate skin around her waist.

"Tyler, Tyler, what are you doing?"

He smiled wickedly. "Why, Lacey, I'm beginning to court you, just like I promised your father I would. . . ."

WHAT ARE *LOVESWEPT* ROMANCES?

They are stories of true romance and touching emotion. We believe those two very important ingredients are constants in our highly sensual and very believable stories in the *LOVESWEPT* line. Our goal is to give you, the reader, stories of consistently high quality that may sometimes make you laugh, sometimes make you cry, but are always fresh and creative and contain many delightful surprises within their pages.

Most romance fans read an enormous number of books. Those they truly love, they keep. Others may be traded with friends and soon forgotten. We hope that each *LOVESWEPT* romance will be a treasure—a "keeper." We will always try to publish

LOVE STORIES YOU'LL NEVER FORGET
BY AUTHORS YOU'LL ALWAYS REMEMBER

The Editors

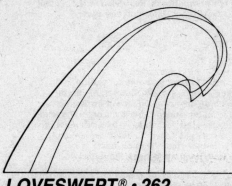

LOVESWEPT® • 262

Sandra Chastain
For Love of Lacey

 BANTAM BOOKS
TORONTO • NEW YORK • LONDON • SYDNEY • AUCKLAND

FOR LOVE OF LACEY

A Bantam Book / June 1988

*LOVESWEPT® and the wave device are registered
trademarks of Bantam Books. Registered in U.S. Patent
and Trademark Office and elsewhere.*

*If you would be interested in receiving protective vinyl
covers for your Loveswept books, please write to this address
for information:*

Loveswept
Bantam Books
P.O. Box 985
Hicksville, NY 11802

ISBN 0-553-21901-4

Published simultaneously in the United States and Canada

---

*Bantam Books are published by Bantam Books, a division
of Bantam Doubleday Dell Publishing Group, Inc. Its trademark, consisting of the words "Bantam Books" and the
portrayal of a rooster, is Registered in U.S. Patent and
Trademark Office and in other countries. Marca Registrada.
Bantam Books, 666 Fifth Avenue, New York, New York
10103.*

PRINTED IN THE UNITED STATES OF AMERICA

O   0 9 8 7 6 5 4 3 2 1

*For Deborah, a very special friend
who's always there.*

Thanks.

One

"Please, Lacey Lee?" the bride asked. Her wedding dress rustled as she slipped into the kitchen where Lacey was putting finishing touches on a tray of finger sandwiches. "Be nice to Tyler. Believe it or not, underneath that disciplined exterior, my ex-husband is a sweet, sensitive man. I want him to feel welcome at my wedding and have a nice time."

Puzzled, Lacey turned periwinkle-blue eyes on her best friend. "Do you think he'll make trouble?"

"Of course not. For the past two years we've acted like we're sister and brother, not ex-spouses. Besides, he and Matt have become friends."

"If you say so," Lacey agreed skeptically, not entirely certain that she believed Callie's claim. But she nodded and gave Callie a warm hug. "Don't worry. I'll give the man the full brunt of my good-old-girl charm." She paused, her impish face lighting up with a mischievous smile. "If I can remember what he looks like," Lacey fibbed.

A small tingle ran down her spine. She'd never

forget. She'd seen Tyler the second he'd walked into the house thirty minutes earlier. Lacey couldn't stop staring at the man. They'd met before, but only briefly, a couple of years ago. She didn't recall him looking the way he looked today—fantastic, in a three-piece suit.

And she didn't recall him staring back at her the way he had today, returning her shocked scrutiny with definite interest. He reminded her of a modern-day Dracula—dangerous, but irresistible. She'd tried to ignore him as she'd chatted with other guests, but she'd remained very conscious of his gaze. Every time she glanced up, his calm, honey-colored eyes were riveted disarmingly on her.

Since she was in Atlanta and, to boot, she was a Southern girl born and bred, Lacey Virginia Lee Wilcox—Lacey Lee to her friends—wryly decided that Tyler was doing a terrific imitation of the charming Mr. Rhett Butler. She only wished she had a fan to hide behind.

"Tyler's changed," Callie said. "He's more relaxed in his old age."

Lacey sighed. "I'll be twenty-five next week. Don't say anything to me about getting older." She paused, thinking. "The last time I saw Tyler he was scowling at me for letting you sell me your van for fifty dollars. After two years, that's what I remember of him—his patronizing smile. He was itching to call me a . . . a hippy . . . or a gypsy . . . something unpleasant, I wasn't sure what."

"Well, you were wearing a man's hat, pink wraparound sunglasses, overalls, and a Save the Whales T-shirt, as I recall. It isn't my fault you two haven't met since. I've tried over and over to get you together." Callie Carmichael pushed a strand of curly brunette hair back into place as she rustled to the kitchen door and peered out into the cavernous living room that had been converted into a floral chapel for her and Matt's wedding. "Oh, dear. You're right. He's frowning. I think he's looking for somebody."

Lacey questioned her old friend's casual attitude and apparent lack of concern, and she felt compelled to say something. "Are you sure that inviting him to your wedding was a good idea? You may feel your first marriage was over a long time ago, but are you certain he does?"

"Lacey Lee, Tyler and I were college kids when we got married. We outgrew each other. He isn't in love with me anymore, and I'm not in love with him. Matt understands the situation, and he wanted to invite Tyler today. Tyler even volunteered to help us make our getaway. Promise not to tell a soul?" she asked, not waiting for a response. "We aren't driving Matt's Corvette on the honeymoon. He's letting everybody decorate it, but we're driving my Fiesta."

"You're going to take the classic? Ruby?" Lacey didn't feel odd about calling the car by the name Callie had given it. Callie named everything—cars, potted plants, farm animals, everything. She'd probably chosen names already for the baby she was carrying. "I wondered about that."

Callie nodded. "Of course. Ruby's hidden. We'll leave in Matt's Corvette, then switch it for Ruby." Callie glanced out the door and back at Lacey. "And . . . eh . . . Lacey, there's another little favor I'd like to ask of you."

Lacey chanced a quick look into the room filled

with guests. She could see Tyler working his way through the mass of people, smiling, chatting, and all the while scanning the crowded hall. "I'm afraid to ask. Does the favor have anything to do with Tyler Winter?"

"As a matter of fact, yes." Callie made an elaborate pretense of checking her refreshment table one last time. "We—Matt and I—would appreciate it if you would drive Tyler up to retrieve the Corvette. Then Tyler will drive it to Matt's house." She smiled beatifically. "I mean, my house. Tyler's sports car is already there."

"Why me?" Lacey was certain that Tyler wouldn't be interested in riding in her lavender van any more than she was interested in driving him in it.

"Because we don't want any of Matt's old buddies to know where we're going. You know how men are at weddings."

"All right," Lacey agreed, trying to appear nonchalant, but she couldn't help worrying. "From here Tyler still seems awfully intense to me."

"You know," Callie speculated, "you may be right. He does seem wound up about something. Maybe you could take him under your wing and entertain him. I'd rather the other guests didn't feel uneasy about his being here."

Lacey gulped. Callie didn't know what she was asking. To Callie he might be like a brother, but to Lacey, the last thing she wanted to do was tempt him. Why, he wasn't even her type. She liked artists and musicians—sensitive, sloe-eyed men who valued serendipitous pursuits and spiritual enlightenment above all else. Tyler was in real estate—big time real estate. She wasn't certain exactly what he did, but she knew it involved prestige, money, and power. Nothing serendipitous.

They had about as much in common as Prince Charles and Madonna. Lacey straightened her shoulders. Callie was her best friend and this was her wedding day, and if Callie wanted her to play nursemaid and chauffeur to an intense, conservative establishment-type guy, she would.

"Sure, Callie," she chirped. "You just get to the 'I do'-ing. I'll wrap Tyler around my little finger."

"Marvelous."

Lacey watched as Callie smothered a smile of victory and hurried out before there could be any further discussion of the great car switch.

Lacey followed her down a long, elegant hallway and stopped to glance at herself in an ornate mirror. Turn on the charm, she told herself. You can do it. She happened to like her carrot-colored hair. She particularly liked its naturally curly look, not because it was stylish, but because it suited her. Honesty and simplicity were things she strived for in every aspect of her life.

Her recycled lavender peasant dress with its laced-up bodice and crocheted trim was strapless and more revealing than she was used to, but she'd loved it the moment she'd seen it in the Nearly New Shop in Atlanta's funky midtown district. Wearing it at this June wedding, with gardenias in her hair, she felt beautiful.

While she was trying to think of lightweight subjects to discuss with Tyler Winter, Lacey moved to the back of the Carmichael living room and found a spot near a large potted ficus tree. She craned her head and looked for him. He was taller than most of the male guests, and she immediately found him in the crowd.

He had a lean masculine build that hinted at strength and an inborn grace. Even across the room, the results of an obviously carefully planned exercise program were evident—a well-filled-out suit and a subdued but healthy suntan. Tyler might not be brawny, but he was most definitely macho, Lacey decided.

Strands of premature gray frosted his warm brown hair, giving him the look of a mature *Esquire* model—the rising executive with a bright, materialistic future, she thought grimly. If his sharply creased navy-blue suit hadn't whispered business, finance, boardroom, he could have been mistaken for a successful athlete—an Olympic distance runner, perhaps. His dark brows were drawn into a straight line now as he scanned the room, still searching for someone. Who? Lacey gasped. Her?

He caught her gaze before she could pretend that her examination of him was an accident. To her surprise he smiled, a lazy, aware smile that said he knew she'd been watching him. With that smile his whole face changed, and she wondered why she'd compared him to Dracula. Pierce Brosnan came to mind as Tyler's left eyebrow arched in a devilish manner.

Suddenly he moved. She'd better think fast because he was heading straight toward her. Surely he wasn't still angry about the van, she thought desperately. Callie had only notified him that she was selling it because she'd never had the title transferred to her. If Lacey hadn't promised Callie that she'd look after Tyler, she'd have turned and made a quick exit out the nearby patio door.

"Good afternoon, Lacey. Nice to see you again.

You're looking . . . different. No overalls. No sunglasses. No whales." He brushed back an errant strand of dark hair that had draped seductively over his quirked eyebrow.

His voice was soft and suggestive, and he came around beside her as if he knew her mad wish to escape. "Hello, Tyler," she managed. Think of Callie, she told herself. Then she said, as steadily as her taut nerves would allow, "Nice to see you too. How have you been?"

"Fine. How's the van?" He took a step closer, and for a moment she thought he intended to wipe a smudge off her nose—with his lips. She wanted to clasp both hands around her unprotected neck. Lacey returned to her earlier opinion. Dracula, yes.

The van. She knew it. He was still carrying a grudge about the van. His businessman's nature had been highly piqued by Callie's low sales price. "Chugging along. I've had it painted lavender."

"If you'd stayed around that day, I would have apologized for being so unpleasant about your deal with Callie. I've never gotten used to Callie's casual attitude toward money, and her decision just took me by surprise."

"Apology accepted," Lacey murmured, amazed at his offer. Just goes to show you that you shouldn't make rash judgments about people, Lacey thought, chastising herself.

"I saw the van in the drive. Lacey's Lovelies? What an interesting logo. Are you providing the entertainment for the reception?" He dropped his gaze to her shoes and let it trail up her body, reading her as if his eyes were his fingertips and she was outlined in braille. When he reached her flushed face, he smiled.

"Not Lovelies, Lovies. Dolls, Tyler. I make one particularly successful line called HuggieBabies." Her words were clipped. He was just trying to provoke her. He wasn't interested in her any more than she was in him. He was just an ordinary man putting a move on a woman. She swallowed hard. Not ordinary. "You make my dolls sound like some kind of nightclub act."

He continued to stand mere inches away from her. Tyler couldn't be intrigued with her, could he? she wondered.

"Of course, Lacey. Dolls and clowns. I'm impressed. I'm sure you're doing very well. Callie has told me that you have a special way of reaching people." He glanced over at Matt, who stood waiting for Callie at the front of the room. "I never thought Callie would remarry," Tyler said.

"But Matt Holland is wonderful. He and Callie seem to be very much in love. They're perfect together." Lacey could have bitten off her tongue as Tyler's brow arched higher. That was no way to keep him calm. It probably hurt him to hear such things about the woman he'd once loved. She cleared her throat uneasily as his gaze burned into her.

"And you, Lacey? Are you with someone?"

"Uh, no. Alone as usual. I'm the eccentric vagabond, as I'm sure you recall."

In the background the soft strains of piano music could be heard. As the music turned into the beginning of the wedding march, Lacey saw Tyler's chest rise and fall in a deep sigh.

She touched his arm sympathetically. "Tyler, I know this isn't easy for you." A disturbing surge of tenderness invaded her emotions. Callie had said he was sensitive, despite his cool and elegant reserve. Hard to believe, she thought, but this man had once been an art student. "Let's be friends," she murmured. "I know you're alone and upset. Just think of me as someone who understands what you must be feeling. Someone who cares." His eyes flickered with deep emotion as he looked at her. In his expression she saw surprise and then . . . mischief? No. It couldn't be.

"I'm not alone anymore, Lacey Lee," he said unexpectedly. "And neither are you. Let's find a good spot to watch," he said softly. "This afternoon, you're with me."

To watch, or to disrupt? she asked herself. Lacey remembered her promise. For Callie she'd keep Tyler calm and distracted at all costs. "Yes," she whispered hoarsely. "Let's."

She tilted her head back and beamed a smile of pure interest at him. Then she grasped his hand and sidled closer to him, intent on keeping his attention away from Callie.

As if grateful for her intervention, he shivered and pulled her inside the circle of one arm then turned her so that her back leaned against his chest. He held her snuggly, and she felt the tautness of his body contract beneath his executive suit. She felt it too well.

The other guests moved forward, making a circle around the fireplace where the florist had fashioned an altar of apple blossoms, sentimental favorites of Matt and Callie's. The crowd pressed Lacey and Tyler tighter together. She couldn't move. She couldn't breathe, either, but that had nothing to do with the crowd.

"*Dearly Beloved*," the minister began, "*we*

are gathered here to join this man and this woman.'. ."

Lacey squirmed uncomfortably. Something about the way Tyler was holding her was disturbing. She remembered Tyler as being reserved, shy even, nothing like the man holding her as if she were a life jacket and he were going down for the third time.

"Are you all right?" she whispered throatily. Lacey tilted her head and tried to look up at him. The scent of his warm skin and expensive cologne washed over her. "You're holding me a little strangely."

"No argument here. I feel a little strange," he whispered back. "I felt it the moment I came into the room. Like a spark just waiting to be ignited. Damn, that sounds so trite. I'm not thinking straight."

"I can understand that. I know you feel sad, but you must try to be happy for Callie's sake."

"Callie?" he asked blankly.

She could tell from the feel of his breath on her hair that he was looking down at her. The music stopped and the crowd became silent. She could hear the irregular beat of his heart in the silence. There was a tightening in his arm. Oh, dear. Lacey pressed herself against him. Anything, she told herself, anything to keep him from making a move toward the bride.

"Tyler, please don't do anything foolish."

"Funny, I've been telling myself the same thing. But I think maybe it's too late."

Her heart galloping, Lacey tried to turn toward him, but he held her firmly. "I want to help you," she urged. "It's all right for you feel hurt, to want to reach out for comfort. I understand."

"You're wonderful," the low, polished voice whispered in her ear. "Hold on to me. Please?" She heard him draw in his breath softly, and for an instant his lips brushed against her cheek.

Lacey stiffened, nodded her head, and held onto his arm. Her fingertips searched out his hand, which was pressed firmly into the center of her waist. She stroked the warm skin soothingly. Caught off guard by her body's languid reaction, she lost track of the ceremony for a moment.

Tyler's other arm slid around her, and he linked his hands firmly. The minister's voice came to her through a haze of sensation.

". . . *to join together this man and this woman*," he intoned. Lacy quivered. Join together? Lordy, she and Tyler were the ones being joined together. She shifted, trying unobtrusively to loosen Tyler's grip without jabbing the woman standing next to her.

"Don't do that," the throaty masculine voice pleaded.

"*Do you, Matthew Holland, take this woman to be your wedded wife, to love and comfort . . .*"

Lacey's curves were pressed into the hard planes of her captor's body with alarmingly synchronized accuracy. She struggled to put distance between their bodies but she struggled with as little fuss as she could manage in the crush of standing onlookers gathered before the altar. She felt an uncontrollable tingle ripple through her, and she tightened her muscles to conceal the shiver, only making the tremor more obvious.

"Lacey, that's enough." His voice was somewhat strained. "The distraction is wonderful but dangerous."

Lacey squirmed once more, then considered what he'd just said. Was she . . . arousing him? Her whole body burned. It was too hot in the room. That was it. She was beginning to feel dizzy. The crowd, she told herself, it was the crowd, not the man.

"Do you, Caroline Melissa Carmichael, take this man . . . "

Tyler was so close. She could smell the fresh, clean fragrance of him. It wrapped around her like a mist blown in from the sea. Lacey felt the ripples running down his body. He was having a physical reaction to the emotion of the occasion, she told herself. She could feel his breath, warm and fast, against her cheek.

His hands moved slightly higher, clasping her midsection just beneath her breasts. She looked groggily down at them. They were firm, well-manicured businessman's hands, feathered with faint traces of dark hair. Lacey shook off an urge to melt against him. He shifted his weight slightly and repositioned his arms, pressing himself even closer. Too close and too far. He'd gone much too far.

She drew her hand to her mouth and tilted her head backward again, covering a hoarse whisper with her fingertips. "What are you doing, turkey?"

"Damned if I know," he whispered, "but I think I'm about to do something even stranger."

"I now pronounce you husband and wife. You may share a kiss."

The groom didn't have to be told twice. He gave a loud whoop and caught his new wife in his arms. The kiss was neither innocent nor short, and the crowd began to laugh before the bride pulled away and looked at her new husband, love radiating from her face.

Lacey heard the sharp intake of Tyler's breath and felt the tightening of his arms about her. When he began to step backwards, dragging her along with him, she couldn't help but accommodate him—step, step, step away from the altar.

"And just where do you think you're taking me, Tyler?"

"Out."

"Why?"

"We both need some . . . air."

Lacey heard the sound of a door scraping open as he shoved a shoulder against it. The heat of the summer afternoon fell over them as they backed onto the patio. Tyler continued to hold her tightly without speaking.

At last Lacey managed to pivot around inside his locked arms, and to face the man who had captured her so possessively and so fervently. They were still close, too close, and they both seemed caught in the spell of the moment.

"You can let me go now."

"Not yet," he said.

"I know this was difficult for you, having been married to Callie and now seeing her promise herself to someone else."

"Hmmmm." It was a noncommittal sound. "When I came here I definitely didn't expect the reaction I'm having. It's a complete shock, Lacey."

"I'm sorry," Lacey said, allowing him to draw her closer. He looked so serious, so emotionally wrought. "Try not to think about Callie, Tyler."

She felt as if she were in the jungle tied to stake, and the tom-toms were announcing her betrothal to some victorious warrior. Me Jane, you Tarzan, she thought in a daze.

He shook his head in amazement. "Where did you get the idea that I'm upset about Callie? She and I have been divorced for almost as long as we were married. I'm thrilled that she finally remarried. I envy her that happiness."

Lacey's blue eyes widened. "Then why did you let me think that you desperately needed . . . soothing?"

He smiled apologetically, his expression serious. "Weddings make me feel sentimental and lonely, and I sensed the same wistfulness in you. I was trying to make you feel better." He paused, and a wicked gleam touched his eyes. "I've never felt anyone better."

The tom-toms had become a twenty-one gun salute. "This strange energy between us is simply a passing mood," she protested. "People do crazy things, caught up in a situation like this."

"Good."

He kissed her then, and she couldn't help but respond. Tyler seemed to need to kiss her, and he kissed her so very well.

The sound of the wedding march from inside the house brought her back to reality. "Oh!" she exclaimed. "I've never . . . I can't believe this!" Without thinking, she shoved Tyler away. The force and the quickness of her movement made him stumble backward against a low banister at the edge of the patio. He faltered there for a moment, striving gracefully to keep his balance. He failed.

Lacey saw the most sensuous mouth she'd ever kissed open wide in surprise. Then she saw the bottom of two black Italian shoes rise high in the air as Tyler tumbled over the banister and out of sight. The last thing she heard was a loud bellow of either pure pain or abject rage from several feet below. Lacey didn't stop to think about what she was doing. She threw one slim leg over the rail and leapt after him.

"Ugh!" She fell about four feet, bouncing off a bed of late-blooming azaleas and landing across his prostrate body, cracking her head into his.

"That's adding injury to insult," he muttered weakly.

Fragments of pain shot through Lacey's skull, but this was no time to consider her own discomfort. Tyler's eyes were shut, and she gasped in fear.

"Tyler, are you hurt?" Little starbursts of light were blinking like neon signs in her vision. Heaven only knew what she'd done to the man beneath her, who was breathing raggedly.

"Oh, Tyler, please open your eyes. Tell me I haven't maimed you!"

"Lacey? Tyler? What are you doing down there on the ground?" Callie's voice was full of laughter as she stood on the patio above. Lacey looked up at her.

"We're just . . ." Lord, what should she tell Callie? How in the world could she explain that this was her way of taking care of Tyler? Callie looked very pleased to see them together, at least.

"Just getting acquainted," Tyler said stiffly, opening one eye at a time. "You enjoy your wedding your way, and we'll enjoy it ours."

Matt appeared by Callie's shoulder and looked down at them. "Rather a public place to get acquainted, isn't it?" he inquired dryly, his voice full of amusement.

"We needed some air," Lacey offered lamely.

"She tried to attack me," Tyler interjected. "It was horrible . . . so humiliating and . . . she made me do things . . ."

"Cut the wisecracks, Winter," Lacey said under her breath. Secretly she felt impressed by his droll recovery. It occurred to her that no other man she'd known would have exhibited such grace under the circumstances.

"I'm about to throw my bridal bouquet," Callie called. "There'll be a crowd out here in a minute. Do you two need some privacy? A blanket? A bottle of champagne?"

Lacey glanced down at Tyler. He shuddered dramatically and formed a martyred expression.

What an adorable fake, she thought. For a nonartistic type, he would have made a wonderful actor. "Are you all right?" she asked without sincere concern.

"I don't know. I can't tell whether I'm lying in a bed of ants or whether I'm feeling the aftereffects of your lovely kiss. But my head is playing hide and seek with the rest of me." He shifted under her. "The next time you want to jump on my bones, I think you could arrange to make it less painful."

"Jump on your bones—hah! Let me help you up." Lacey realized how bizarre they looked—him flat on his back, her sprawled on top on him with her knees between his legs. She pushed herself away and knelt beside him. "Take my hand and smile. We've got to get out of here quick, before all those women come out to catch the bridal bouquet Callie's about to throw."

"Just don't let her throw it at me. I've had quite enough of violent women today." Tyler tried valiantly to conceal a grimace as he allowed her to help him to his feet. When he draped his arm over his shoulder, she could tell he really needed the support. He swayed, but gallantly smiled up at Callie and Matt.

"The wedding was lovely," he offered, "but I think Lacey and I will skip the bouquet toss, if you don't mind. Won't we, Lacey?" He gave a soft groan and nudged Lacey forward.

"I'm thrilled to see you two together, but Lacey is supposed to prepare our going away box of cake and refreshments from the reception," Callie protested.

"And Lacey is going to drive you up to the shopping center to bring the Corvette back," Matt added with an amused tone in his voice. "You do remember that you're supposed to handle the car, old buddy," Matt reminded Tyler. "Remember, the Corvette, the one covered with balloons and old shoes?"

Callie made no attempt to hide the laughter that was ready to bubble out at any moment. "We wouldn't disturb you, but we really can't drive that on our honeymoon."

Lacey and Tyler looked at each other helplessly. Neither Callie nor Matt realized that he'd fallen off the patio and was hurt.

"Can you walk to the van?" she whispered.

Again, he set his face in a dramatic expression of sacrifice. "I think so, if you'll help me."

"I suspect that you're not quite as injured as you'd like me to believe."

"But you can't be sure, now, can you?"

"Okay, Mr. Winter, okay. You've touched my guilty streak. I'll help you to the van, then I'll fix Callie and Matt's going away box and come back to you. Unless you think you're well enough to handle this alone?"

He groaned. "I don't think I'll be able to drive . . ."

"That's what I figured. I'll drive. Where's Ruby?"

"Stashed up at Town Center Mall. Matt and Callie are going to slip out early, and we'll meet them there and drive the wedding car back."

"Well?" Callie called cheerfully from the patio. "What about it, you two lovebirds?"

Lacey heard the other guests making their way outside so Callie could throw her garter to the unmarried groomsmen and the wedding bouquet to the single women. Lacey knew that Callie had planned to see she caught the bouquet, and she also knew Tyler had discombobulated her so much, she couldn't have caught water in a hurricane.

"Just a second, Callie," Lacey called out. Tyler was injured. He probably needed to be checked by a doctor. But she couldn't let them know that and ruin their wedding.

"Go drink punch and cut your cake, you two," Tyler said cheerfully. "Lacey and I aren't interested in garters and wedding bouquets. At the moment we have . . . other things on our minds."

They ducked around the corner of the house, past Matt's white Corvette . . . now covered with Just Married streamers and hung with crepe paper and tin cans, to the safety of Lacey's lavender van. She opened the side door and shoved a mound of brightly colored dolls aside. He climbed in gingerly and sat down on the carpeted floor.

"Oh, Tyler! You're bleeding." She'd hit him in the nose, as well as the head. Now bright red drops were making tiger paws down the front of his shirt.

"Just a minor inconvenience, Lacey. Don't worry. I'll just sit here in the van and quietly bleed to death until you get back."

"Oh, poor thing."

In the back of the van Lacey found a scrap of soft cotton cloth for Tyler to use as a handkerchief. From the drink cooler she always carried—for those long days spent on the road between craft shows—she filled the cloth with ice.

"Tilt your head back and hold this ice on your nose until I get back," she instructed as she slid out the van's side door.

"What about Matt's car? We promised Callie we'd pick it up." Tyler's face etched with concern. "We can't leave a classic Corvette in a shopping center parking lot."

"I'll drive you to get the car. I owe Callie that much." Lacey eyed the blood-spattered man who looked more like the victim of a wrestling match than an elegant Dracula, as she'd thought earlier.

"Do hurry," Tyler prodded, settling himself down in the back of the van. "I wouldn't want the world to think I've tried to kill myself over the wedding."

"Good heavens!" He was right. Suppose someone did see him? She got back inside the van, drew all its bright lavender print curtains closed, then left hurriedly out the side door again.

"Just let me fix Callie and Matt's food and I'll be right back. In the meantime, consider the van as an ambulance and stay put! I'll take care of you."

"Oh, I'll stay put," Tyler said solemnly, stretching himself out on a pile of stuffed animals, "but do hurry. I was already overheated and this ambulance isn't air-conditioned. I'm desperately in need of care."

She put her hands on her hips. "Sorry about the heat. I don't need air-conditioning ordinarily. My dolls don't mind the heat and neither do I." Tyler's color was pinking back up. He wasn't seriously hurt, and they both knew it.

"Say, you don't have a pillow, do you?" he asked.

"Take one of the clowns. They're soft. That's why they're called Lovies. And don't move until I can get back to see what you need."

"My needs are very great, Lacey."

"Yes. I'm sure."

"I'm not moving an inch. I wouldn't dream of passing up intensive care," Tyler promised, adding under his breath, "not with a Lovie in a lavender van."

Lacey gave him a rebuking look and shut the van door. A Lovie in a lavender van. What an irrepressible flirt this man was. Maybe she'd like to learn more about him. She shook her head at her strange attraction to a bleeding businessman.

Two

"But it was only a nosebleed, Lacey. I don't think I need a doctor," Tyler said with a groan. "If you'd just stay with me for a while . . ."

"Are you always this persistent with a woman?"

"Actually, no. I almost never am. But you're unique."

She didn't know what to say to that apparently sincere remark, so she kept silent. Lacey drove the van down the Carmichael's crowded drive and out into the street. At this point she wasn't sure what she ought to say, feel, or do about Tyler Winter. Nothing was going right, including the insane temptation she was fighting—the temptation to pull the van over and play tender nursemaid to the man bleeding all over her lavender carpet.

"You need a doctor," she said firmly. "You may think you're all right, but I'm not taking any chances. The way my afternoon is going, you'll probably faint, and I'll have to perform mouth-to-mouth resuscitation."

"Ummm. That's not a bad idea," Tyler drawled. "Mouth to mouth is much more promising than head to nose."

Lacey felt her face flush. She remembered all too clearly the shape of his mouth and the gyrations of her own lips in return, just before she came to her senses and shoved him. She shook her head. What was wrong with her? She understood men and ordinarily had no trouble remaining on pleasant, platonic terms with them. But again, Tyler wasn't ordinary.

She'd simply gotten carried away by her emotions at the wedding. That was why she'd behaved so peculiarly, but now she was back in control again.

"Direct me to where we're supposed to meet Matt and Callie and pick up the car," she said crisply.

"No need to hurry. Callie and Matt are still cutting the wedding cake."

"Maybe," Lacey voiced skeptically, "but the way Matt was hurrying the photographer, I think they're going to get away faster than they'd planned."

"Can't say I blame him." Tyler took a satisfied breath. "I like being alone with my lady too."

"Directions, Tyler. And I'm not your lady."

"Town Center, and that's too bad. Cut down Roswell Road to Route Seventy-five north. They'll meet us at the gas station in the front corner of the lot. We shouldn't have any trouble spotting a white Corvette covered with balloons and tin cans. You can check my vital signs while we wait."

"The only vital sign I want to see is the one that

says Town Center." Lacey tried to ignore her passenger's gleeful flirting. "I'm surprised they'd leave Callie's Fiesta convertible parked there for five minutes, much less all this time."

"Oh, the station manager has it inside. Under lock and key," Tyler explained. He sighed with exaggerated sorrow. "Like your heart."

"Like my—"

"Correction: You're a heartless gypsy."

"You're an unimaginative yuppie."

"Ah, she wounds me," he said, undaunted. "I grew up poor and lived my youth as a starving artist, haven't you heard? Doesn't that draw a tiny bit of compassion into your narrow perspective?"

"You sold out. You gave up art for business."

"I discovered that I liked being able to pay my bills."

"I pay my bills and my family's bills too. We gypsies aren't irresponsible, you know."

"Family?"

"It's a social unit comprised of closely related human beings. Like parents."

"Why do you support them?"

"They're artists. They need their space."

He groaned. "Oh, no, you're a Valley Girl gypsy. Need their space? That's a typical artist's cop-out for 'They don't know how to make a living, so they stay at home and create.'"

"I misjudged you, Tyler. For a few minutes during the wedding, I thought you were human."

"I'm sure your parents are great people. Let's stop picking on each other."

"Fine," she agreed.

At the next traffic light, Lacey stole a glance

into the back of the van. Tyler's eyes were closed, and he grimaced as he took the square of cloth, which was dripping with the melting ice, off his nose and put it down on the carpeted floor of the van. His nosebleed seemed to have stopped.

Looking at the man was a mistake. He'd removed his jacket and vest and unbuttoned his blood-spattered shirt to his waist. She could see the swell of his chest as he breathed, and Lacey was surprised at the amount of thick dark hair there. She was even more surprised at the insane desire she had to touch it. Lacey tightened her grip on the wheel and drew her gaze back toward the road.

"Lacey . . . you know this is terrible."

"What's terrible?"

"In one afternoon, you've totally destroyed my image and turned me into Bozo the Clown. I don't understand myself."

"Neither do I, but I think I like Bozo much better than the Executive Man."

"Well, I don't. Where are we, anyway?" His voice was cool, too cool, and Lacey knew that he, too, was having second thoughts about their weird interlude.

"I don't think it's much farther," she said, then lapsed into an uneasy silence. He wasn't the only one who'd changed during the afternoon. She tried to close off the train of thought their conversation had taken, concentrating instead on her driving. The wedding was behind her, and in a little while she'd have fulfilled her promise to Callie. Tyler was fine. He'd go in one direction and she'd go in another.

Lacey knew this part of suburban Atlanta well.

Her family home was nearby. She winced as she recalled Tyler's remarks about her parents. Alfred Lee and Gynneth Wilcox were charming and she loved them dearly, but she silently admitted that they were genteel ne'er-do-wells, old-world hippies. Their home had once been a plantation, Harmony Hall. Sherman, the dirty devil, had burned the house during the battle of Atlanta, but her great-grandfather Powell Lee Wilcox rebuilt it and managed to keep it in the family.

"What are you thinking?" Tyler finally asked.

"Oh, I'm thinking about war."

"Hell, we're not about to do battle again, are we?"

Lacey laughed. Better to revert to fun and games. She could relate to comedy better than confessions. "Actually, I'm thinking that Callie is as sentimental about Ruby as I am about my lavender van."

"Well, it brought her and Matt together. If he hadn't wanted to buy it, they'd never have met. Do you think we'll feel that way about this van one day?"

"Not likely." His dogged pursuit was unnerving. Unnerving, and oddly enjoyable. Lacey scowled. "Why should we?"

"I'm growing rather fond of it and the crazy lady who drives it too." With that statement, Tyler came to his knees and slid between the bucket seats to sit up front beside her.

Earlier she'd convinced herself that he was only a man she'd hurt accidentally, a source of embarrassment, a moment's diversion. Now, with him sitting so close beside her, she knew that he was much more. He was formidable. Her body felt like a yo-yo on a string. Somewhere back there among the dolls, Vincent Price was directing her torture.

Her deep thoughts took her attention away from her driving, and she had to jam on the brakes to avoid hitting the car in front.

"Laceeey!" Tyler lurched forward, only catching himself at the last moment.

"Sorry!" The last thing she needed was for him to hit his nose again. The bright red drops of blood on his shirtfront stood out enough already. She was liable to be arrested for assault if a policeman saw him.

"Wouldn't you like to stop and take off that shirt?"

Tyler jerked his head around. "Well, I don't know. What did you have in mind?"

"I had in mind getting rid of the evidence of my crime before Callie and Matt see you. I can't imagine what they'd think."

"Don't worry, Lacey," Tyler said, chuckling. "I won't tell them how physical you get. And if we're stopped by the police, I promise I won't them that I've been abused."

"Oh, Tyler. All kidding aside, I am truly sorry about what happened. We're bound to reach the mall before Matt and Callie. I'll just run into a shop and buy you another shirt. That way they won't worry."

"If that will make you happy. Personally, I liked the disrobing idea better."

Town Center Mall loomed up on the right, and Lacey took the next exit. The sprawling mass of buildings, some still under construction, covered acres. Lacey found a shop with an outside entrance, pulled into a parking space opposite it, and left the motor running while she ran inside.

The shop was a boutique housing novelty items and colorful goods from foreign countries. With a glint in her eyes, she quickly skimmed the racks. Tyler hadn't always been stiff and downright stuffy. Callie had said that in college he was a free spirit, a tie-dyed peace marcher with an open-minded *joie de vivre.* And now he was sitting outside in her van with his shirt half off. Did she dare?

She did. Lacey made her selection and darted back to the van. "Here you go, sport, a fresh shirt. Get changed and we'll buzz over and wait for Callie and Matt to arrive."

"Shucks, ma'am." Tyler looked around the deserted area where she'd parked . . . and grinned. "I thought this was a taking-off, not a putting-on spot."

"Don't be coy. Put on the shirt. By the time we get to the service station, Callie and Matt ought to be there."

"Okay, if you're sure that you wouldn't rather jump into the back of the van and give an injured man a helping hand with his problem."

"You don't need a hand, Tyler. You appear to be superefficient and you don't have a problem."

"Oh, I have a problem, all right."

"What kind of problem?"

"A problem with why I find your red hair and lavender outfit such an enticing combination. I think you must be a sorceress, Lacey Lee. It isn't just that weddings are so emotional. I've been to plenty of weddings, and I've never started thinking the kind of thoughts I've had ever since I walked in the door today and saw you. It's very strange."

"It's the lick on the head, Tyler. You're spacey."

"I must be, and clumsy too. Will you help me? I can't seem to get this cuff link unfastened."

Lacey leaned across the gear box and took Tyler's hand, stretching it across her knee while she studied the studs. There must be a secret to unfastening them, she surmised, but she couldn't see anything on the back of the stud to release the top half.

"How'd you get them on?"

"I didn't. I lost one of my old ones and bought these on the way to the wedding. The store clerk inserted them in the cuffs."

"Great! Let me see the other one." She pulled his right arm around until he was almost straddling her knees, with both arms stretched across her lap. She slid forward.

"Damn, Tyler, I can't see an answer." His nearness was making her all thumbs. She concentrated on the cuff links, trying to ignore the fact that his bare chest was only inches from her face. "Can't you slide your arms through the shirt cuffs without removing the links?" In exasperation she lifted her face, right into the vicinity of Tyler's.

She froze, statue still, and licked her bottom lip unconsciously. They were so close that her tongue accidentally touched his upper lip, and she tasted the salt from the perspiration beaded there. She closed her eyes in embarrassment and sucked in a breath of surprise. This time when he kissed her, her response was so natural that she hadn't realized she'd parted her lips until his tongue invaded her mouth.

"Hey! You in there!"

Lacey jerked back. She had her elbow pressed

against the van's horn and hadn't even noticed its blaring alert. Neither had Tyler, apparently. It was incredible. Outside the window a burly construction worker was hammering on the side of the van.

Lacey was aware of the feel of Tyler's bare chest against her dress and the burning sensation his kiss had branded on her mouth. The heat joined with the flame in her cheeks. She turned to the window, rolled it down, and looked at the curious construction worker.

"I'm so . . . so sorry," Lacey stammered. "I just pulled in here so my friend could change his shirt."

"Sure, lady. Right here in broad daylight. I don't know what to think about some people. And you're not even kids!"

"Let's go, Lacey," Tyler said cheerfully. "I don't think you want to add a public indecency charge to the day's strange events."

"Public indecency! Tyler Winter, bite your tongue. This is all your fault."

Lacey quickly backed the van out of the parking space. With a squeal of the tires she started out, whipping the van around the mall to the area where they were to meet Callie and Matt.

"There are scissors in the sewing basket, Tyler," Lacey snapped. "Just cut your cuffs open. I'll pay for the shirt."

Tyler grinned, gave her a half salute, and crawled into the back of the van. A few snips of the scissors and the shirt was gone, balled up and planted beneath the mound of dolls.

Tyler crawled unself-consciously back to the front again, seemingly unaware of the shiver he invoked when his bare upper arm grazed Lacey's shoulder as he slid by. "What did you buy for me to wear?" He reached inside the plastic bag and pulled out the replacement shirt. "Dear Lord. You took revenge on me again."

"What do you think?" Lacey had a hard time keeping her lips straight. She didn't dare look over at Tyler as she absorbed the utter silence of his contemplation.

"It's awesome, simply awesome," he managed, and began to put the bright lavender T-shirt over his head. He smoothed the front of the shirt, erasing any wrinkles from the design painted in glowing colors.

Stamped on the lavender shirt was a sad looking clown with bright carrot-red hair and a downtrodden expression. Written across the bottom in brilliant green letters was the slogan Clowns Do It in a Funny Way!

He sighed. "Injured *and* humiliated. Is there no compensation for all my suffering?"

"Not the kind I suspect you want." Lacey couldn't help grinning as she scanned the parking lot. "Look. Callie and Matt are turning in." Lacey parked the van alongside the newlyweds. Tyler slid out the passenger door and walked casually around to greet Callie and Matt.

Callie took one look at Tyler and burst into disbelieving laughter. "Where on earth did you get that shirt?"

"This is Lacey's van and Lacey is a lady with a mission," he answered solemnly. "She furnishes a badge of honor to all survivors of her quest. Sort of like raising the flag after the battle, you know."

"Maybe," Matt chortled. "Looks like the war was interesting."

"Well," Lacey interrupted, "I guess you two want to claim Ruby and get going." She nodded to them, then to Tyler. "I think I can safely say good-bye now."

"What do you mean?" Tyler asked in alarm. "We have to take the Corvette back to Matt and Callie's house."

"You drive the Corvette. I'll drive my van. I have to run a couple of errands and hit the road to a craft show."

"Oh!" Tyler swayed and caught the door of the van to steady himself. "I'm sorry. . . . I seem to be dizzy."

"Are you sick, Tyler?" Callie asked anxiously.

"I hope not," he said with careful gallantry. "It's as if someone hit me in the head. But don't worry. You two take off. I'll get the Corvette back."

Lacey bit her tongue and gave Tyler a look that would have burned a broom-sage patch.

"Are you sure you're all right? Have you got the flu?" Matt asked. "You look awfully pale."

"I'm fine. It's just a headache. I don't know what could have caused it."

The idiot was faking. Lacey knew he was faking. There was nothing wrong with him. She ought to let him make a complete fool of himself. She ought to, but one look at the concern on Callie's face and she knew she'd have to control herself. Callie and Matt deserved to have a wonderful, carefree honeymoon.

"I'll take care of Tyler," she said sweetly. To him she muttered, "Come on, clown, let's get into the Corvette. I'll drive you home and have someone bring me back for the van later."

Tyler quickly jumped into the Corvette and ensconced himself with his head laid back dramatically against the seat and his eyes closed.

"Go on, you two," Lacey assured Matt and Callie. "I'll see that your car is safe. I make no promises about Tyler, however."

Matt lifted Lacey over the low-slung door into the Corvette's driver's seat. "Don't mess up this work of art by opening the door," he said seriously. "Callie's father is going to slip over and take more pictures before he removes the decorations, so just leave it like this when you get it to our house."

"Thanks again, you guys," Callie said warmly. "Everything went just the way I'd hoped it would." She bent to kiss Lacey's cheek and whispered in her ear, "But I am a little worried about Tyler. He'd acting strange, very strange."

"I heard that," Tyler grumbled. "I'm just a poor lonely businessman in need of affection." He turned his head on the Corvette seat and smiled devilishly at Lacey.

She made a small sound of disgust, but inwardly she realized that she was having a wonderful time.

Lacey drove slowly away from the parking area, her emotions in a confusing whirl. This man was downright aggressive, but he was also funny, sexy, and not at all as solemn as she'd thought earlier in the day. The whimsical artist still lurked underneath his *Esquire* exterior, she decided. How interesting.

"You can stop the act now, Tyler."

"I don't know," he answered in a stricken voice. "I still feel pretty shaky."

Mild annoyance zinged through her. "Don't try

to con me, you faker. There's nothing wrong with you, and you know it."

Tyler straightened up, leaned very close to her, and whispered in her ear, "I'm not so sure about that, Lacey Lee. I think something may be very wrong. I'm wearing a battered nose and a ridiculous shirt, but I'm feeling terrific."

Her answer was drowned out by the cheerful honking of a pickup truck that pulled up alongside of them at a traffic light.

"Whooowheee! Kiss her, man!"

Lacey gave the truck's three rowdy occupants a curt look. "How come she's in the driver's seat?" one of them called. "You gonna let her wear the pants, man?"

Tyler shook his head pleasantly. "I don't want her to wear any pants at all."

"Tyler!"

The men guffawed loudly. The one nearest them jabbed a finger out the open window at Tyler. "Look at that shirt! Man, where'd you two get married? The Church of What's Happenin' Now?"

"Auuugh!" Now it dawned on Lacey why she and Tyler were drawing attention.

Tyler gave the truck passengers a thumbs up sign and grabbed her in his arms, crushing her against him. Then he kissed her again.

The kiss may have been for show, but by the time the light changed and the cars behind them began honking, Lacey knew that her face and her hair were the same color. This time she didn't have an explanation for the furious pounding of her heart or the irregular contractions of her chest muscles.

"What the . . . What do you think you're doing?"

she shrieked. She jerked away from him, changed gears, and stomped the Corvette's accelerator. A strand of pink streamers came loose because of the frantic motion of the car.

"Relax, Lacey. Don't you know how to have fun? Besides, I wasn't the only one doing the kissing. Your lips were pounding, throbbing, aching, grasping—"

"Not grasping," she corrected dryly. "I was trying to bite you."

She refused to acknowledge that he was right about her response to his kiss. "Don't let my off-guard, spontaneous reaction to your brutish masculine charm go to your head," she urged. "Are you feeling stronger now?"

"No, actually, I'm feeling pretty weak. Must be from losing all that blood. Perhaps I have a slight concussion."

"Indeed," she said without conviction.

"Yes. And you know what they say about concussions, don't you?"

"No, what do they say about concussions?"

"That you can't let the victim go to sleep. You're going to have to keep me awake, Lacey. Just to be sure I'm all right."

"I'm going to do better than that, Tyler. I'm going to make certain that someone is with you straight through the night."

Tyler smiled lazily. "I knew you'd assume responsibility and do the proper thing. We could go to my place and— Why are you turning here?"

"Because this is the hospital, Tyler, where there is an emergency room with round-the-clock intensive care." Lacey pulled the car into the parking space by the emergency clinic's front door and killed the engine.

"Ma'am, you can't park here," a security guard said as he ambled over.

"Isn't this where you come when you have an emergency?"

The guard looked at the Corvette's Just Married sign, at Tyler's strange combination of pin-striped slacks and lavender T-shirt, and back at Lacey. "Even a hospital can't help some people. What kind of emergency do you have?"

"It's my wife," Tyler began woefully. "The idea of being married has unhinged her, I believe. She hit me in the head. Then she shut me in the back of a van . . ."

"Not quite," Lacey began, rolling her eyes. "What actually happened—"

"She's abusing me, sir," Tyler said wistfully, "and I've done everything I know to make her happy. I mean, hell, I let her drive. I'm prepared to let her carry me over the threshold. I'll give her my maidenhood without shedding a tear. I ask you, how equal can a man be?"

"Well, buddy, you may have an emergency, but this isn't the loony bin. I don't think we can do anything to help you here. Now move this car."

"Wait just a minute, please," Lacey implored. "I am not married to this man, and the reason I've brought him here is that he hit his head. He's been behaving oddly ever since. I think he may have a concussion, and unless you want to open yourself up to a law suit, I suggest you get someone to bring a wheelchair."

"Whatever you say, lady," the guard said, shaking his head. "Anybody who'd get married in a purple T-shirt must have something wrong with his head anyway."

Tyler allowed himself to be placed in the chair and rolled into the emergency room. He kept his face casually covered with one hand, and Lacey couldn't tell whether his nose was tender or he was hiding a smile. Probably both, she suspected. Either way, she intended to make sure that he got the care he deserved.

"Patient's name?" the admissions clerk asked.

"Tyler Winter."

"Tyler William Winter," Tyler corrected solemnly.

"Date of birth?"

"I don't know his physical age, but his mental age is about twelve." Out of the corner of her eye, Lacey watched Tyler being rolled into a curtained examination area.

"Address?"

"Sorry, I don't know."

"Mrs. Winter, I know you're worried about your husband, but could you be a bit more cooperative?"

"I'm not Mrs. Winter and I don't know anything about this man except that he hit his head and had a nosebleed."

"All right. How did the accident happen?"

"Well, actually, it was after he kissed me. I gave him a shove, and he fell off a balcony. Then I jumped over the balcony after him and bumped him in the nose."

"Of course. You pushed him off a balcony and you dived after him and hit him again?"

"I know it sounds crazy," Lacey admitted, "but that's how it happened."

"And what did you hit his nose with?"

"My forehead. Of course, I hit the rest of him too, but that didn't bleed. At least I don't think so; I haven't taken his clothes off."

"Was this before or after the wedding?"

"After, but . . . ma'am, I am not involved with this man!"

The woman behind the counter jerked her head up and frowned. "I don't know what kind of prank you're trying to pull, but I think I'd better call someone to talk to the patient. Maybe he knows what happened. Just have a seat over there."

One look at the guard lounging about the doorway told Lacey she'd better do as she was told. The admissions clerk was behind the curtain with Tyler for several minutes. When she returned to her station she covered her mouth and whispered to the other women in the office. One by one they glanced up at Lacey and smiled.

That was enough. Lacey started down the corridor toward the emergency cubicle, intent on telling the examining doctor that the whole thing was a joke that had gotten out of hand. She'd apologize properly, beat Tyler around the head, and leave.

". . . and that's the truth," Tyler was telling the doctor. Lacey stopped outside the curtain, her ears tuned. "There really isn't anything wrong with me. But if I let her get away from me, I may never find her again. She's one special lady, Doc. How about helping me out?"

"And exactly what do you want me to do?"

"Tell her I need to be watched for the next twenty-four hours, or something like that. That I'm not sick enough to be hospitalized, but I shouldn't be left alone. She'll have to stay with me. I have a little score to settle with her anyway."

"Ahem. Mr. Winter, this is very unusual." The doctor was silent, as he considered Tyler's request. "We'll see."

Lacey hurried away before the doctor walked out of the cubicle. She sighed, thinking of Tyler's disturbing words about her, then began to smile. If Tyler wanted to play games, he had picked a champion opponent. She hid her smile as she went back to the examination area and entered through a part in the curtain. Tyler lay on a white-sheeted gurney, smiling and humming. He stopped immediately and assumed his injured-lover expression.

"Tyler, I'm so sorry," she murmured. "I honestly thought you were faking the head injury." Lacey came to the side of his bed and brushed the hair away from his forehead. "Can you ever forgive me?"

"Sure, gypsy. I know you didn't mean to hurt me."

"The doctor says that you may need watching. They're going to x-ray your head, and then if everything is clear, I'm going to take you home for the night."

"Ah, Lacey, that's so nice of you." Tyler caught Lacey's fingertips and brought them to his lips, kissing them lightly. "I promise I won't be much trouble, and I'd love for you to see my condo. I've been redecorating it and it's finally done."

"Oh, I'd love to see your condo, Tyler." She felt his mouth move sensually beneath her fingertips. All afternoon she'd wanted to touch him, and now she gave in. With her other hand, Lacey slid his T-shirt up and ran her fingers through his chest hair. "How do your ribs feel?"

His chest quivered. "Oh . . . a little sore. A massage would be nice."

"Hmmm. Of course."

His ribs felt fantastic, Lacey thought distractedly. The hair that covered them was soft and feathery. "I promise I'll look after you. But first you have to have the X rays, then we'll get out of here."

"Fine," he whispered. "I'm ready."

"Not quite. The nurse wants you to take off your clothes and put on a hospital gown." She'd already spotted a gown folded up on the gurney next to him.

"Take off my clothes? You've got to be kidding. Why should I take off my clothes?"

"Hospital rules, Tyler." Lacey let her fingers trail down his stomach and away.

He sighed. "Oh, how could I refuse?" He began to unbuckle his belt—a sleek, black eelskin belt with a handsome gold buckle. "Would you like to help?"

"You might say that."

He stared at her curiously for a moment. "Are you sure this is a good idea, Lacey? Here?"

She shrugged, went to the other gurney, got the gown, and handed it to him. "I suppose I can't . . . take care of you . . . with so many people around." Lacey leaned down and kissed him lightly. "I'll wait outside. Just yell when you're done."

"You could help. I'm not bashful."

"Later," she promised, and left the enclosure in a rush before she broke into peals of laughter.

Lacey wasn't surprised at how quickly Tyler undressed and called for her to come back. The blue hospital wrap made him look much taller, its short length falling just above his well-formed knees. The calves of his legs were delightfully hairy, and he had big, angular feet. She couldn't help admitting that she'd never known the sight of a man's feet to have an arousing effect on her, but Tyler's did. Lacey scanned the flimsy gown. She'd probably picked up a garment designed for a woman. It was perfect.

"You put it on backwards," she pointed out.

"Ah. I see. What do you think?" Tyler asked, catching at the closing of the green outfit that threatened to fly open and expose suntanned legs and a great deal that she suspected wasn't suntanned. His pained expression was gone, and now there were golden flecks of color dancing in his honey-brown eyes.

"I think you'd better be very still, Tyler. Obviously the designer of these little numbers must have been told that the purpose of the garment was to keep the wearer immobile."

Lacey took his slacks and T-shirt, draped them over her arm, and smothered a new smile. "I'll tell the nurse that you're ready for your X rays. You just wait right here. And Tyler, I want to thank you for one of the most exciting days I've ever spent. You're one very special man, every inch of you."

"You ain't seen nothin' yet," he promised.

That's what her poor deprived and confused heart was afraid of, Lacey thought as she walked down the corridor past the admissions desk and out of the emergency room. She had to get away from him and his outlandish ways. The temptation she felt was too great.

She climbed into the balloon-covered Corvette and drove straight out of the parking lot, ignoring the peculiar looks of the emergency ambulance personnel by the door.

All in all, she thought, it had been a lovely wedding.

• • •

When Lacey told Callie's father what she had done, he laughed, plied her with left-over refreshments from the reception, which they stored in her cooler, and drove her back to reclaim the lavender van, promising that he'd check on Tyler on his way home.

Lacey would spend the night at the warehouse she maintained in the back of a friend's fabric shop in a small town in the mountains and spend tomorrow picking up the new prototype dolls that were being made by her employees in their homes. The dolls were good. She had a feeling that the new soft doll, each one an original in the image of its owner, would be a hit. In fact, she'd already had a call from one exclusive toy store about carrying the dolls. But her mind definitely wasn't on the business at hand.

Repeatedly Lacey's eyes were drawn to the suit pants and the clown T-shirt in the back of the van, and she thought of the man who'd worn them. She tried to recapture some of the amusement she'd felt as she drove away from the hospital, but all she felt was a growing sense of depression.

She felt drained, uneasy. Just let down after the emotional high of the wedding, she told herself. Even the smell of wedding cake gave her a feeling of disquiet. It was Tyler. She couldn't get him off her mind. He really had been a good sport, so different from the Tyler she'd remembered. He hadn't been stiff and formal. He'd been—well, terrific. Fun.

The entire afternoon had been fun, and she was honestly sorry that she hadn't stayed around to watch him as she'd promised. There wasn't anyone special in her life; she hadn't had the time for a relationship. She'd been just like Callie, Callie who hadn't been interested in a man until Matt came along and wouldn't let her go. Lacey was beginning to feel a little sorry that she'd done the proper thing. Poor, beautiful, sensual Tyler, lying there on the gurney with his long, beautiful legs exposed, wearing only a skimpy gown. He must be furious with her.

She was beginning to be furious with herself.

He'd probably come after her with a shotgun.

He'd probably take her out on some deserted dirt road and abandon her.

He'd probably take her clothes and let her walk home.

He probably wouldn't even kiss her first.

He probably— Oh, hell, he'd probably gone home and forgotten all about her.

Three

Tyler waited anxiously for the return of the nurse, the doctor, Lacey, somebody—anybody! Lacey was the anybody he most wanted to see. It was as if she'd cast a lifeline to him today, a lifeline that could rescue him from the brusque and serious world he inhabited. He didn't want to be set adrift again.

There was constant activity in the corridor outside Tyler Winter's cubicle. He could hear the soft squish of nurses' shoes as they scurried back and forth, the constant sound of the hospital intercom summoning technicians and doctors, and the whooshing sound made by the door to the waiting room, but nobody came to see about him.

Eventually a police officer stopped by to inquire whether or not he wanted to press charges against the woman who'd attacked him and pushed him over a balcony. He thought of Lacey waiting somewhere in the hospital to take him home and comfort him, and explained to the patrolman that it had all been a misunderstanding. He felt very gallant.

The officer shrugged his shoulders and left. No one else came near him. He was half-naked in a skimpy hospital gown that didn't begin to cover him decently, and he'd been abandoned. By the time the emergency room doctor pulled back the curtain, he knew he'd been had.

"Sorry, man, I got caught up in a problem and lost track of time. Didn't anybody tell you that you could go home? Where are your clothes?"

"Lacey said I had to have X rays before we could leave," his voice trailed off in barely contained fury. "This wasn't your idea, was it? Your nurse didn't tell my . . . uhmmm . . . friend, Lacey, that I had to undress and put on this skimpy gown, did she?"

The doctor squinted at the chart he was holding, rocked back and forth, and looked abashed. "Well, now. It seems we have a problem. Your . . . friend apparently made all the arrangements to have you admitted. And then she left."

Tyler finally had the full picture. He'd planned to trick Lacey into going home with him; instead she'd turned the tables. "Why, that scheming woman!"

The doctor couldn't control himself. He began to grin.

"She's stolen my clothes and my transportation!"

The doctor's grin turned into a full belly laugh. "Yep. Looks like you've been outfoxed. And she left you the bill too."

Tyler sprang to his feet, felt the skimpy gown fly open, snatched it together, and sat back down. Nothing like this had ever happened to him before. He was a dignified businessman, dammit. He belonged to the chamber of commerce. The doctor was still chuckling. "Find me something to cover my . . . assets!" Tyler ordered. "And get me out of here!"

Within twenty minutes a snickering staff, the security guard, and the emergency room technicians had managed to scrounge up a set of operating room greens and a pair of abandoned slippers.

Red faced, Tyler explained the mistake to the head of the hospital's accounting department and arranged for his company to verify his ability to pay—when he got his wallet back. He was headed toward the exit, intent on calling a cab, when he spotted Callie's father walking through the doors.

"Where is she?" Tyler made no attempt to conceal his fury from his ex-father-in-law, Wesley Carmichael.

"She's gone, son. She sent me to rescue you. How's the head?"

"Better than hers will be when I catch up with her. What's her address, Mr. Carmichael?"

"Can't help you with that, Tyler. I have no idea where Lacey lives. She just turns up now and then. Maybe Callie knows, but you'll have to wait until she and Matt get back from their honeymoon to find out."

"Do you know where they've gone?"

"Not unless they call in. They didn't leave an itinerary."

Tyler sighed, rebuking himself silently. Had he lost so much of his old romantic spirit that he'd actually consider pestering Callie on her honeymoon for a petty reason like this? "I don't know what I'm thinking of," he muttered.

"I believe I do," Wesley Carmichael said, smiling a knowing smile. "I've seen that same look on Matt's face, but I'm sorry. You'll have to wait. Lacey did send you this." He handed Tyler his wallet, his watch, and his ring. "Simmer down, boy. You'll find her."

"Oh, yes," Tyler agreed with a vengeance. "With the resources at the office, I'll find her. I'll find her and then I'll, I'll . . ."

Mr. Carmichael laughed, then said seriously, "I wouldn't make any rash threats, Tyler. Some women are special—very special—and maybe you ought to think twice before you do something you'll regret."

Still, as Tyler followed his former father-in-law to his car, he was already planning his method of revenge. He'd steal Lacey's funky van and paint it black. He'd steal her and hide her in some remote mountain cabin with no clothes and no firewood. He'd make her put an embarrassing hospital gown on that luscious body of hers, then he'd send strangers in to snicker at her. . . .

It was hopeless. There were one hundred and seventy-two Wilcoxes in the metropolitan Atlanta telephone directory, and there wasn't a Lacey in the bunch.

After two days of dialing, Tyler gave up on finding Lacey before Callie and Matt returned from their honeymoon. He knocked on his partner's door and went inside, and with a deep sigh he eased down in the blue leather chair adjacent to the desk.

"You look like hell, Tyler," Win Maxwell observed

wryly. "I haven't seen you for two days. What happened? Big wedding hangover?"

"No, not exactly. I met somebody."

"She must have tied you up. Who was it, Spider Woman?"

"No, more like a female wrestler. She shoved me over a balcony and gave me a bloody nose."

"Nothing you didn't deserve, I'll bet."

"No. Yes. I don't know. All I know is that I've lost her."

"So? Find her."

"I can't."

"Well, there's a whole ocean out there, sport, cast out another line. You've always been a great fisherman."

"Yeah, I know. Hell, I hate to admit it, but this particular trout is a keeper." Tyler wasn't a stranger to simple sexual attraction. He recognized it for what it was, and his feelings for Lacey didn't fit in that category. She wasn't stunningly beautiful, and she certainly wasn't interested in him. But every time he closed his eyes her bright, cheerful smile kept coming at him.

"I see. Well, get your mind off her and give me a hand. You remember that property up in Roswell? The one that we granted the second mortgage on?"

"Sure. I remember. Melody Place, or something. What's the problem?"

"Harmony Hall," Win corrected. "It's in default. They're three payments behind, and bookkeeping can't get any response. The phone has been disconnected, and the couple who owns the place won't answer our notices. This is a choice piece of land—big bucks, Ty. I think you'd better take a run up there before we start legals on a foreclosure."

"Sure," Tyler agreed. "Might as well do something useful."

"I have to warn you. I worked with the wife when I was setting up the mortgage. She's a flake. In fact, my impression was that her whole family is ready for a cereal box. Weird, old Southern aristocracy gone bohemian. Can you believe that everybody in the family's name is Lee."

Tyler sat up. "What do you mean?"

"A bunch of artists—unsuccessful artists—with no money and even less business sense."

"No, I mean how do you know they're all named Lee?"

"They're all listed as beneficiaries on the insurance clause: Alfred Lee Wilcox, Gynneth Lee Wilcox, Medina Lee Wilcox, Arthur Lee Wilcox, and Lacey Lee Wilcox."

"Lacey?" Tyler vaulted to his feet. "Wahoo! That's her, partner. That's the girl I met. Thanks. I'm out of here."

Artists, Win had said. Tyler considered that interesting tidbit as he drove. Lacey's family were artists. Tyler let his mind flow back through the years to when he'd first met Callie. He was a penniless college student existing on government loans, a struggling young artist who dreamed of displaying his work in famous galleries one day. He had talent, at least his teachers had said so. What was more important at the time, however, was that he also had a bitter need for immediate financial security, the kind that a career as an artist wasn't likely to provide. He'd given up art for business.

He didn't paint anymore. He hadn't in years, not since his divorce from Callie. Why then did he have a sudden urge for a blank canvas and the smell of paints and linseed oil? Dammit, it was all tied in with Lacey. She'd turned his whole life upside down. Even as he drove he found his gaze flickering across the traffic in search of a pixie of a woman with carrot-colored hair, driving a lavender van.

"Mother? I'm home." Lacey balanced a tray of hors d'oeuvres in one hand and a box containing a section of wedding cake in the other as she backed up the steps and into the spacious old kitchen. "Mother?"

"I'm right here, my darling. Why can't you call me Gynneth like everyone else?" The dark-haired, serene looking woman kissed her daughter's forehead, took the cake box, and searched for an unoccupied spot on which to put it down.

Lacey looked around the kitchen in amazement. Shells were strewn everywhere—large shells, small shells, and shells that smelled suspiciously as if their residents were still in residence. The entire kitchen smelled like the beach at high noon.

"Because," Lacey answered as she shoved one section of what appeared to be animal bones aside and deposited the tray of sandwiches, "I'm your daughter, not one of your artists. This is supposed to be a kitchen, Mother. What is all this?"

"Phillip's shells. He's a designer."

"What does he design, mollusk graveyards?"

"Jewelry, Lacey. Jewelry made from shells and bleached animal bones. You'll love Phillip. He's

just come back from a tiny island in the South
Seas."

Lacey took another deep breath and tried not to
gag. "How do you prepare food around all this
art?"

"Hmmm . . . I guess we are going to have to
relocate these shells, aren't we?"

Lacey loved the reference to *we*. What her mother
meant was that she expected Lacey to handle the
problem. Solutions weren't her mother's forte.
Problems simply weren't supposed to happen, and
when they did she closed her eyes and found some
new idea to focus her energies on, leaving the
problem in Lacey's capable hands. Sometimes
Lacey felt like an extra in that Jimmy Stewart
movie, the one about the giant, invisible rabbit.
Life wasn't real at Harmony Hall.

"I think I have the answer." Ignoring her mother's squeal of horror, Lacey began sweeping shells
into paper bags and boxes. "In case you hadn't
noticed, I brought some food for your—guests. I
suppose you have a full house, as usual?"

"Actually, my dear, we're a bit overcrowded just
now." Lacey's father wandered into the kitchen,
looking like a young version of Colonel Sanders,
in Bermuda shorts and a Hawaiian shirt. His eyes
lit at the sight of the finger sandwiches. He hugged
Lacey affectionately.

"Hello, Daddy."

"*Bonjour*, sweetness. Phillip is bunking on the
couch in my den, but I refuse to accept his shells in
there. Hmmmm, food. Gynneth, love, why don't you
call the liquor store and have them send over a nice
bottle of wine, something that will go with these
sandwiches and—good heavens, wedding cake?"

"Wedding cake?" Gynneth echoed in surprise. "Where did you get wedding cake?"

"At a wedding, Mother. I've been trying to tell you."

"Lacey! Did you get married and not let your own mother know? First your sister elopes to New York to live with a guru, and now you? We have this lovely house and neither of our girls gets married here."

"Mother! This food was part of what was left from Matt and Callie's wedding. I've had it in my cooler, on ice, but the sandwiches are probably stale by now."

"Wedding cake would really be better with wine," Alfred insisted. "Maybe I'll call the liquor store."

"Speaking of calling someone, Mother, why has the phone been disconnected?"

"I'm sure I don't know," Gynneth said sincerely as she lifted her head and looked suspiciously into the box Lacey had deposited on the counter. "Probably some computer mistake. I've been meaning to drive down to the bank and inquire, but with the annual meeting of the Daughters of the American Revolution coming up, I simply haven't had the time. I'm the chairwoman, you know."

Lacey let her mother's words circle around in her mind for a moment. Computers? Bank? More often then not there was enough sense in her mother's ramblings to solve a problem, if you could just put the pieces together.

From somewhere in the huge, old house came the sound of African fertility music, interrupted by the clatter of what sounded like a herd of reindeer heading toward the kitchen. Through the din came the onslaught of canine barking in the front of the house and a loud masculine call for help.

"Gynneth!" *Tappity tap tap.* "Gynneth!" The reindeer turned out to be Spence, the aging resident tap dancer, who had a habit of spacing his words to the rhythm of his feet.

"Beowulf and Miranda"—Pause. *Tap.*—"have some yuppie type"—Pause. *Tap.*—"cornered on the porch"—Pause. *Tap tap.*—"in a dreadful fright."

"Oh, dear." Gynneth sighed. "Probably another of those bill-collector persons. Lacey, will you be a dear? Find out what he wants? By the way, Lacey, where is your new husband?"

"Mother!" Lacey shook her head and made her way through the cluttered house to the front door. She pushed open the screen and stepped outside. "I'm very sorry about the dogs, Mr.—? Lordy! I don't believe it. Tyler?"

Tyler Winter was perched on the porch rail as Miranda, the toy poodle, tugged valiantly on his left pant leg, and Beowulf, the ancient Great Dane, who had his two front paws propped on the railing, slurped a large pink tongue up the side of his face. Lacey gasped.

"Miranda, let go this minute. You naughty dog! Beowulf, off the porch, right now!" The two animals reluctantly retreated.

It couldn't be. She'd left Tyler at the hospital, never expecting to see him again. She was suffering from hallucinations. Ever since she'd kissed the man, she hadn't been able to get him out of her mind. Every time she closed her eyes, she saw him lying on that gurney in that indecent smock with his magnificent legs exposed almost all the way to their inception.

"Lacey? Is it really you?" Tyler was studying her in disbelief. "I've been looking everywhere for you." Tyler left his perch on the railing and dropped lightly to the floor.

"You really looked for me?" She was surprised, and her voice reflected it.

"Oh, yes," he answered grimly. "Didn't you think I would, after your cute little trick? Why did you run away?"

"Oh, dear. I had to pick up some supplies from my warehouse yesterday, and for the last two days I've been making the rounds to the houses of the ladies who sew for me. I'm sorry, Tyler. Here, let me . . ." Lacey reached out, intending to brush Great Dane fur off the shoulder of the magnificent gray suit he wore.

"Oh, no you don't. Stay away from me, Lacey Lee." Tyler held up both hands in warning and glanced back over his shoulder at the porch railing. "What is it with you, porches, and balconies? It's one thing to get your jollies by pushing people over them, but to steal your victim's clothes and desert him in his hour of need, leaving him to the mercy of not only the hospital staff but the police? I'll bet you kick your dogs too."

"Police?" Oh, no! Tyler was angry, very angry. She couldn't blame him. "Are you all right?"

"Yes, except for my wounded pride and my embarrassment. I'm all right, or at least I was, until I got here."

"And now?" She moved toward him. Up close he didn't appear too angry. In fact, if she hadn't known better, she'd have thought that he was amused. His eyes had turned a hazy brandy color, with little slivers of silver where the gold flecks had been the day before.

Everything went still as Tyler gazed back at her. He was having as difficult a time breathing as she was, she realized.

"I hope you got home all right," Lacey murmured. "Callie's father said he'd come for you."

"You know, it wasn't the fact that you stole my clothes and left me with everything exposed to the world in a damned skimpy gown—"

"You were pretty sexy in that gown."

"I could have understood that. It wasn't that you led me on and embarrassed me in front of the rest of the world. I realize I asked for it. But," his voice dropped to a whisper, "you and I were working on something good, Lacey Lee, and you walked away from me without a thought."

"Without a thought? Hah! I wish. Believe me, I've thought about you. I haven't thought of anything else for two days, and I finally figured out why. It was the wedding, Tyler."

"Are you sure?"

"Aren't you? I mean, weddings always make people emotional, don't they? Everybody kisses everybody at weddings, don't they? I mean, it's an emotional time."

"Yes, it must have been the wedding. People do get emotional at weddings, particularly when they've had a lick on the head. That could account for someone behaving in a totally illogical manner, couldn't it?" He moved a step closer. He was saying the words, but his expression didn't indicate that he believed any part of his own explanation.

"True." She caught her breath. "Then we both understand what happened at the wedding."

"Yes. We understand. The emotion of the moment made me kiss you. Several times."

"It was simply a matter of cause and effect. That same emotion made me push you away. I never meant for you to fall over the balcony and I certainly never meant to give you a bloody nose." Her heart was pounding, and she felt as if she were an underwater diver who'd just used up the last of her oxygen.

"But we're not at a wedding now, so why do I have this overpowering urge to kiss you again?"

"I don't know, Tyler." She lifted her head and parted her lips.

He kissed her again. It really was the necessary thing to do. She'd wanted him to from the instant she saw him, and it was exactly like she remembered it, as she hoped it would be, as she wanted it to be. She kissed him back, thoroughly and completely, with a talent she hadn't known she possessed.

The screen door squeaked open. "Oh, Alfred," Lacey dimly heard her mother croon. "I knew it. He's the groom. She kept him waiting out here while she told us what they'd done."

Lacey stepped back quickly, blushing. Gynneth stepped forward, smiling. "Hello, Mr. . . . ? What is your lovely name? I suppose I should make the first move. I'm Gynneth. Gynneth Lee Johnston Wilcox, of the Savannah Johnstons. Please, don't call me Mother. I simply refuse to be that old."

The confusion on Tyler's face was not an uncommon reaction from someone seeing Harmony Hall and meeting the Wilcox family for the first time. Surrounding him like a living presence was a shabby antebellum mansion. Giant magnolia trees swayed gently in the front yard. The African fertility music that flowed out the front door underscored the scene like a bad sound track for a B movie.

"Mother." Lacey tried to catch her breath and speak sensibly. "I told you that the wedding cake was from Callie's wedding. This is Tyler Winter. Years and years ago, he and Callie were married."

"Well, that's nice, dear," Alfred said. He shook Tyler's hand vigorously. "Ever so much nicer if everyone is friendly about divorce. Very modern attitude, though I never quite understood that sort of thing myself."

"We've never had a divorced person in the immediate family, have we, Alfred darling?" Gynneth asked. She turned toward Tyler. "But then, practically everyone has been married by the time they're fully grown in today's world, haven't they? Except our dear Lacey, who seems to have been saving herself. Although there have been men . . . I particularly liked the Norwegian flute player—"

"Norwegian flute player?" Tyler interjected.

Lacey stifled a groan. Her mother went on talking. "But I can't think that I've ever heard of using wedding cake from a first wedding in a second wedding. Have you, Alfred darling? Well, never mind, it's probably much more common than I'm aware. Why did we never divorce, Alfred? You know, I don't think we ever thought about it."

"I don't know. I rather think we're well matched, my dear," Alfred answered. He shook Tyler's hand. "Good show, my boy. I'm Alfred Wilcox, Lacey's father. Welcome to the family."

"Thank you, Mr. Wilcox, but—"

Barefoot and bare chested, Lacey's brother took that moment to wander onto the porch. Arthur

Lee grabbed Lacey and kissed her cheek. "Hello, sister dear, didn't know you were back from your craft show."

"Arthur," Gynneth chimed, "meet your sister's new husband, Tyler. The naughty girl got married without letting any of us know."

Behind Arthur came the limber-legged tap dancer. He completed his routine with what looked like a painful split, right by Lacey's feet.

Lacey's head reeled. She knew Tyler must think they were all completely bonkers. She'd grown up with her totally irrational family, a mother who wrote poetry and researched the family history for the Daughters of the American Revolution, and a father so obsessed with the life of his ancestor, Colonel Robert E. Lee, that he'd added Lee to his wife's and children's names.

Arthur, her twenty-four-year-old brother, really was a wonderful musician, but his genius seemed fated to remain unproven. Her sister, Medina at least had managed to leave the nest for the New York stage. Never mind that she had settled with her guru-lover into an apartment in Soho, and that the closest she'd come to fame was dancing in an off-off-Broadway production of *Hair*.

Arthur smiled. "You don't look like the sort of fellow Lacey would pick, Winter, but welcome to the family anyway." Arthur extended his hand and waited for the confused Tyler to shake it.

"Thanks," Tyler ventured, "but—"

"Sweet Suffering Je-hosh-a-phat!" Lacey exclaimed in disgust. She put her hands on either side of her head. "You're crazy, you're all crazy. I'm sure that Tyler must think he's stepped into the Twilight Zone. Tyler is *not* my husband. We're not married. He'd only . . . just . . . a friend."

"Oh." Gynneth seemed nonplussed for a moment, then brightened. "Alfred, Lacey's finally brought home a friend, a young man. She's never done that before, has she? How lovely and old-fashioned, Alfred. They aren't called suitors anymore, they're called friends. Well, he'll just have to bunk with Arthur. We simply don't have another spot for a guest."

"Mother—"

"I'm sorry, darling," Gynneth said. "You're right, we're being terribly rude, but we understand. We know how shy you are about men. If you want to call him a friend, then we'll comply. Get Tyler's luggage, Arthur."

"But, Mother," Lacey said, trying to explain as she fell helplessly in at the back of the line of people following her mother, "Tyler isn't spending the night."

"Nonsense!" Gynneth trilled. "Of course he is. After all, you do want us to get to know him, don't you? I mean, how else will we be able to give our approval? You all come along and we'll make this a very special occasion. Perhaps I'll write a poem. Come along, Alfred, Arthur, Spence. Let's leave these two young people alone."

Lacey stopped and turned back to face Tyler, who was still standing wide-eyed on the porch. "I'm sorry, Tyler. It will take me a while to straighten this out. My family is a little—different. They think they've gone bohemian, but they're really terribly old-fashioned."

"I can see that," Tyler said dryly. "It certainly makes it easier to understand your lavender van and those clowns and dolls, to say nothing of balconies and bloody noses. Insanity obviously runs in the family."

"Oh, no. They're not responsible for what happened at the wedding. You mustn't hold them responsible for my kissing you, or bloodying your nose and then abandoning you. I'd never kissed a stranger in my life, but now I've done it four times in four days."

Tyler caught her hand. "I thought it was me who kissed you, at least in the beginning. Later," his lips quirked as he tried to hold back a smile, "later, I'd say it was a mutual undertaking, a very nice mutual undertaking."

"Well, it was a mistake. I'm sorry I embarrassed you, and I'll be glad to take care of the hospital charges."

"I tried to find you, Lacey. I wanted to, but Callie's father didn't know where you lived. Everyone I spoke to said you live in the lavender van."

"Only when I travel the craft show circuit. How did you find me?"

"I didn't. Well, I did, but . . . let's just say that I'm here."

"But why are you here? I don't understand."

"Well . . . because—" He broke off. What was he going to do? How could he possibly explain? If he told her he was there because his firm was about to make her family homeless, she'd never forgive him. He looked at Lacey's face, all flushed from the kiss they'd exchanged, and made up his mind. There had to be another answer to the problem of Harmony Hall, but he would focus on finding it later. For now, all he could think about was that he'd found her, Miss Lacey Lee who made clowns to bring smiles to children and bought crazy T-shirts to brighten up the disposition of a man who was much too stern.

Tyler cleared his throat roughly. "Because I was looking for you. Do you know that there are one hundred seventy-two Wilcoxes in the telephone directory, and you aren't one of them?"

Confusion mixed with another more unsettling emotion made it hard for Lacey to concentrate. He'd looked for her. After the terrible things she'd done to him, he'd looked for her. Not only that, but Tyler had met her family, and he hadn't yelled, screamed, or left in a huff. He was still standing here, staring at her with his stormy eyes. He was one remarkable man. He was one sinfully sexy, calendar hunk, and he was standing on her front porch in the late afternoon shadows looking as if he expected to be ravished—and she was standing there wishing she could comply.

"Thank you, Tyler," Lacey said softly. "I'll try and explain to my family that you aren't my beau. I do like you, but as you can see, you'd never fit into this circus I call a family. You'd better leave while you can."

"Lacey!" Arthur called, "I'm moving the duck off your bed. Mother says for you to bring your suitcases in and get ready for supper."

"Duck?" Tyler's laughter couldn't be contained any longer. "I can't stand it. Do I really have to go? I like you, Lacey Lee Wilcox, and I'm hoping that we can be more than just friends. Do let's go up and have a look. I can't wait to see the duck in your bed."

"Don't be ridiculous, Tyler," Lacey snapped. "I have no intention of letting this go any further."

"I'm never ridiculous, at least I've never been until I met you. Now it seems to be a recurring problem. And what's even crazier, I think I'm beginning to like it."

"Tyler, we can't be more than friends. We aren't even friends."

There was a long moment of silence. "You could pretend. I don't have to."

Lacey Lee Wilcox had always considered herself able to handle anything. After all, as the only normal member of her family, she'd had years of practice. But explaining Harmony Hall to a man dressed in a pin-striped suit, a man who could have stepped out of a ten-most-eligible-heavenly-bachelors' list, turned her bones into quicksand and her mind into oatmeal.

Helplessly she looked around, seeing her home through Tyler Winter's eyes. Why hadn't he already turned and run? The porch needed paint, the roof sagged, the gazebo was falling down, the barn was little more than a shell and its copper rooster weather vane had fallen over so that the rooster appeared to be crowing upside down.

Only the porch's wicker furniture looked decent. The brightly-colored cushions she'd stitched were still in good condition. Beyond a patch of too long grass in the front yard, she could see masses of daisies and daylilies blooming profusely. They'd taken over the flower beds and were racing wildly out of control into the woods. Nothing she could see gave any indication that the very precise, businesslike man standing before her would fit in. What was he doing here?

"Well," she faltered. "I . . ."

"Well, what?"

There was a tiny crinkle at the corners of his lips. His eyes caught the sun's late-afternoon rays and lit up with a kind of secret amusement, paralyzing her with their warmth.

"Why are you here?" she demanded softly. This man wasn't stuffy. He was wonderful. She wished she were wearing a dress instead of a long print skirt and a Georgia Wildlife Federation T-shirt. She wished he were her beau.

Tyler decided that he couldn't avoid the truth any longer. "Actually, I'm here on business. But if I'd known Harmony Hall was your home, I'd have come for personal reasons."

"Business?" she echoed blankly. "Real estate business?"

Tyler hedged. "My firm is interested in . . . acquiring Harmony Hall." Well, that was the truth.

"What?"

"Look, couldn't we talk about it later? After dinner? Maybe tomorrow when I've had a chance to make friends with those two attack dogs that cornered me earlier?"

"After dinner? Are you sure you want to? I mean, when my family cooks a meal it could be anything from Mandarin muskrat to Siberian shish kebab. And by the way, they'd both taste the same."

"I'll chance it. And after dinner, we'll talk."

The screen door slammed as Arthur stepped out. "Lacey, if you and your friend don't want to listen to Mother's latest ode, you'd better make a quick exit."

"Oh, good heavens! Quick, Tyler, follow me." Lacey quickly went inside. She climbed the great, curving staircase at a clip. This was really getting out of hand. Instinctively she headed for her bedroom in the turret. It was the only place she was safe. She didn't stop to consider her actions because she'd always taken refuge there when her mother went on one of her creative binges.

Too late, Lacey realized. They reached the top of the stairs just as Gynneth called from the bottom. "Wait." She walked majestically to the center of the bottom step and nodded to her husband and to Lacey and Tyler. Standing on the step above Lacey, Tyler assumed a blank expression and stared at Gynneth solemnly.

"May you come to know and share what my Alfred and I have found," she said, looking from them to her husband.

"Now, Tyler," Alfred said, "you must tell us your intentions. Old fashioned, but still a lovely custom."

Gynneth nodded her head and beamed her approval.

Lacey felt like crying with embarrassment. "Oh, good grief. Mother, Daddy. This isn't a formal declaration of intent. We're just going into my room to . . . talk. Tyler, pay no attention to them." Lacey turned to climb the last step and nearly crashed into him. He was laughing silently. Tears were running down his cheeks. "Why . . . why don't you help me explain?" she sputtered.

"Far be it from me to tempt fate, your mother, and my guardian angel." Tyler looked down at her with a strangled expression of mirth on his face. Then he glanced at Lacey's father. "My intentions, Mr. Wilcox, are most certainly to do the honorable thing. I intend to court your daughter with all haste."

"Tyler, you can't . . ." He was serious. Pulling Lacey up beside him, he clasped her arm under his elbow and, like a grand Victorian gentleman taking his lady for a stroll in the park, he directed Lacey through her bedroom door.

Lacey clung to Tyler's arm and inhaled the overpowering male scent of him as he slid his other arm around her and held her close. The door, unbalanced and loose on its hinges, swung shut behind them with a heavy thud.

This was crazy. Tyler Winter had been infected with the Wilcox virus. Not only did he not panic over the family's idiosyncrasies, but he'd begun to behave just as bizarrely. She could see it now, in a bulletin at the monthly chamber of commerce meeting: "*Young Business Executive Wanders into Eccentric Old Family Hall and Goes Totally Bonkers.*"

"Tyler, turn me lose."

"Hah." He lowered his mouth toward hers.

Not again, she begged silently. Too late. She was being kissed. She didn't know what this man intended, and leading her family to believe that they were sweethearts was dishonest of him, but there was nothing dishonest about what he was doing with his mouth. Tyler finally drew back and grinned down at her in undisguised joy.

"Tyler," she protested. "You don't know what you're doing."

"You're absolutely right, and it's been a long time since I've felt so good about ignorance. Kiss me, Lacey."

"I won't," she said, but her refusal died a quick death as his mouth captured hers again and his tongue slipped deliciously inside. She was only vaguely conscious of him pushing her down on the bed and lying beside her. "Oh, Lordy," she whispered.

"Oh, Lordy," he echoed, his fingertips following the curve of her backside. His hands came around to her rib cage, then slid under the T-shirt and cupped one of her generous breasts. He sighed.

"I knew you'd feel this wonderful, Lacey."

"Tyler, Tyler, what are you doing?"

"I'm beginning to court you. I have your father's permission."

Lacey barely knew this man. Nothing Callie had ever said about the college-aged Tyler Winter described the mature man who was making her feel such wonderful things.

"But we're not sweethearts, Winter," she cried, making a valiant effort to regain control. "Why are you doing this? We're not lovers. We don't even know each other."

"But we're going to be lovers, darling." He started kissing her again. "We're going to be much more. There's no way I'm going to let anything happen to interfere with this courtship." He kissed her deeply.

"Hello in there!" A knock of the door was followed by its opening and a subsequent gasp. Lacey looked up to meet the startled eyes of a boarder. "Hello? I'm sorry to interrupt, but has anybody seen my duck? I left it in here on this bed."

Lacey tore herself from Tyler's arms and sat up, hastily straightening her T-shirt and the skirt that had somehow ridden up her thighs.

Tyler simply rolled over on his stomach and buried his head in the covers. His shoulders shook. From the curious sounds he was making Lacey thought at first that he was choking.

"I s-say, I'm very s-sorry, Lacey," the pudgy, balding man in the doorway said. "I didn't know anyone was in here."

Tyler rolled over on his back and threw up his hands in mock defeat. "He's looking for his duck,

Lacey. Would you have any idea where the man's duck might be?"

"I don't know," she said wearily. "But, given everything else that's happened today, I'm sure that it's around here somewhere."

Lacey looked helplessly at the confused man in the doorway and at Tyler, who was now convulsed in another fit of laughter. Why couldn't she have had a normal family—a mother who made meat loaf every Thursday night, and a father who worked on an assembly line or in an office?

"I've never had so much fun in my life," Tyler said between breaths, wiping his eyes. "By all means, let's help the man find his duck." Tyler straightened his tie, tucked his blue oxford-cloth shirt back into his wrinkled pin-striped trousers, and inquired seriously, "What color is your bird, sir?"

Four

"You have a lovely home here, Mrs. Wilcox," Tyler said with genuine interest in his voice. "How have you managed to hold on to it? I mean," he quickly added, "with all the shopping centers and office parks being built around here?"

"Oh, Gynneth figured out the answer," Alfred Wilcox said proudly. "It was her idea to turn Harmony Hall into an artists colony—pool our resources, so to speak. It's worked out rather well, hasn't it Lacey?" He cleared his throat by taking a long swallow of iced tea, then smiled pleasantly at his wife.

They were sitting on the side porch in the darkness. The dinner dishes were still unwashed in the kitchen, but Lacey knew better than to suggest that she excuse herself and begin clearing them away. *Worked out rather well*, her father had answered. Lacey wanted to hoot. Her mother and father lived their lives as though their mutual inheritances had not been drained years ago. They

67

acted as if their bank account automatically replenished itself and servants took care of mundane household chores. Somehow both those expectations were fulfilled.

The chores managed to get done, even when Lacey was on the road. Her parents never realized that they would go under financially in a minute, if it weren't for the very creative bookkeeping she did when she came home between trips. The problem was getting harder and harder to handle, however.

Darkness was a welcome relief to Lacey. Her face continued to burn as she remembered what had transpired in her bedroom before the hunt for Mr. Spragg's duck. Mr. Spragg had found it outside, but the search had broken the chain of events, and Lacey was still reeling from the possibilities of what might have happened if the sculptor hadn't interrupted them.

How on earth could she have let herself fall into fanciful delusions more typical of her mother? In the past she'd been able to call a halt to a situation before it got out of hand, but not with Tyler. For a time she'd let herself be caught up in the fantasy that she and Tyler actually meant something to each other.

She closed her eyes. She didn't want to think about him anymore. Why was he acting so awkward about his business here? His firm wasn't the first to try and buy the Wilcox property. Situated outside of Atlanta in the burgeoning Roswell area, Harmony Hall was prime real estate. So far, though, he hadn't mentioned to her parents that he wanted to buy the place. He seemed anxious to ignore business for pleasure. Of course, they'd refuse his offer, but Lacey was confused. Everything she'd ever heard about Tyler portrayed him as some kind of stiff, no-nonsense workaholic. Maybe the lick on the head she'd given him had genuinely addled him. He actually seemed to be enjoying the misunderstanding about their relationship. Courting. Ridiculous! He wasn't fooling her. All this silliness was simply for her parents' benefit.

"I suppose we did jump to conclusions about you and Lacey being married, Tyler darling," Gynneth agreed with a touch of disappointment, "but I honestly don't see why you can't spend the night. You could sleep in Arthur's room. He has twin beds and the extra bed isn't being rented at the moment."

Lacey brought herself abruptly back to the present. "Mother, Tyler is not spending the night. He has a business to run, a *real estate and investment business*," she emphasized, giving him an opportunity to explain his mission.

"Of course he does, Lacey," Alfred intoned. "Your mother and I understand. We know you young people would rather be together than sit out here with us, so why don't you go along and take a walk. Mother and I'll do the dishes." Alfred Wilcox stopped his rocking and leaned forward, holding his pipe in one hand and his crystal goblet filled with iced tea in the other, as he waited for Tyler's answer.

"Thanks, Mr. Wilcox." Tyler stood up in the darkness. "We'd appreciate that. A walk would be nice—after we've done the dinner dishes. Coming, darling?"

"Darling? I mean dishes?" Lacey corrected herself quickly.

Earlier Tyler had removed his coat and vest, and traded his blue oxford-cloth shirt for one of her brother's pale-yellow polo shirts. He held out one hand to help her out of her chair.

"You're volunteering to help do the dishes?" Lacey asked. Even the crickets stopped chirping in astonishment. Lacey was accustomed to the residents of Harmony Hall conveniently disappearing after a meal, just as they'd done tonight. She certainly wasn't used to having a man offer to do kitchen duty.

"Certainly. Then we're going to take a walk in the moonlight." He waited, his hand still extended with patient confidence. "Let's go, gypsy. We have a few unsettled matters to discuss."

"We do? Why?"

"Why do the dishes? Because"—he reached out and caught her hand, then drew her to her feet—"because they're dirty. Why take a walk?" He whispered in the vicinity of her left ear, "Because I like talking to you, Lacey Lee Wilcox, and I want to know everything about you. I like touching you. I like you touching me. And I want to kiss you again, very much."

Lacey heard her mother say, "I'm so glad they aren't already married, Alfred. Don't you think a garden wedding would be prefect? The garden used to be so lovely this time of year." Lacey walked numbly into the house, with Tyler right behind her.

Tyler and her mother were definitely two kindred spirits, she realized. He appeared to understand Gynneth, and that was unreal. In fact, Tyler seemed to understand her family better than she did. She needed to put a stop to the situation before Tyler began to believe all her mother and father's nonsense.

Tyler slid his arm around her waist and pulled her close to him in a teasing way as they walked down the hall. "I promised your father that I was going to court you, but I'm afraid that I'm not terribly experienced with courtships. You're going to have to coach me. Holding hands and kissing are okay, aren't they, Lacey?"

They walked into the kitchen. It was blessedly dark, and Tyler's arms were determined as they clasped Lacey around her lower back, drawing her to him before she had a chance to object.

"Wait, Tyler," she begged. "I think we ought to talk. This is getting out of hand. The wedding was nice and so were the fun and games afterwards, but now it's gone too far."

"You're right. We need to talk, and we will . . . later," he whispered, and she could feel the trembling of his lips as they touched hers. "Where'd you get your red hair?"

You're making a mistake, she tried to say. She knew she ought to stop him. She'd been telling herself that all evening. While she and Gynneth had prepared the evening meal, she'd thought about nothing but Tyler and how she was going to handle his continued presence. She'd tried diligently to explain their relationship to her mother, but Gynneth, being Gynneth, saw his romantic pursuit as not only perfectly proper, but expected.

Finally Lacey had given up on explanations. *Nobody* seemed willing to hear the truth. And the most disobedient person in the entire household was the one being held inside Tyler's embrace, being kissed by Tyler's lips, molding herself against Tyler's body like pliant clay on a potter's wheel.

"Red hair?" she murmured vacantly. "From my great-grandfather. Where'd you get your bulldozer personality?"

"Not from my grandfather. He was a bum. Ah, Lacey," he whispered as his lips played down her neck and back to her mouth again, "don't ask for explanations. I don't have them. For the first time in a very long time, I'm operating on pure emotion. You've captivated me, enchanted me, cast a spell on me. I think you've turned a stern frog into a carefree prince."

His lips could have demanded anything, and she'd have been powerless to refuse. He could have swept her up in his arms and taken her back upstairs, and she couldn't have stopped him. But he simply kept kissing her—light, teasing, haunting kisses that made her ache.

At last Tyler lifted his head and looked down at her in the darkness. "You've made me feel something I thought I'd lost completely," he said softly.

"I can't imagine you'd lose anything you wanted to keep," Lacey said tightly. She made a weak attempt to pull herself away, but her body was like marshmallow cream in his arms.

"I lost you once, but I don't intend to make the same mistake again. I'm not a careless man, Lacey, not about what I want. I'm not sure yet where our relationship is going, but this time I'm not going to explain it away or mess it up by examining it. I think something very good is happening between us, my vagabond lady, and you have to feel it too."

She could feel it. It was strange and wonderful. "Don't be silly," she managed to say. "You've just gone from the emotion of a wedding to being caught up in the Wilcox family craziness. It'll pass."

"I hope not, Lacey Lee Wilcox. Do you realize what it means to have a real family, a family that cares about each other and supports each other? I adore your family. But the member of your family that I adore most is you."

"Tyler, is it really you talking? Somewhere between the *I do*'s and the nosebleed, I must have taken a lick on the head too. I'm Lacey, remember? Lacey, the vagabond woman who drives a lavender van and travels the craft show circuit? You can't possibly be serious. You . . . This is dumb, Tyler, just plain dumb."

"Stop arguing, Lacey."

Whatever else she might have said was swallowed up by Tyler's lips as he kissed her again. It was the gentleness, the restraint in his passion that inflamed her own. His holding back touched her with such unexpected warmth. She felt as if she were reaching out to him, as though he were the sun and she were coming out of cold darkness to be surrounded by gentle heat.

Lacey shivered and let herself relax. Foolish? Yes! Wonderful? Definitely! She knew she was making a mistake and yet she couldn't seem to stop. Her arms circled around his neck and her fingers worked through his thick dark hair. She never wanted this moment to end.

"Darling." He was gently pushing her away, separating himself from her. "Duty first, remember? The dishes?"

"Dishes?" Her voice was thick.

"I know, sweetheart. Boy, do I know, but this isn't the time or the place. I think we'd better get to those dishes before I go beyond courting and get to the consummating. I'm not partial to kitchen tables, myself."

Tyler walked across to the sink, rested his clenched hands on the countertop, and stood looking out the window for a moment as the sound of his uneven breathing filled the shadowy kitchen.

Lacey watched his back move away in a blur.

"I'm traveling in uncharted waters, Lacey, and I don't want to mess up."

"You're only volunteering to wash the dishes, Winter, not navigate the Okefenokee Swamp." Lacey switched on the kitchen light, flooding the room with garish brightness. She blinked at the glare. This was what she needed, no shadows to soften the obvious or make what was happening seem like a romantic adventure. Total exposure was what she wanted.

"Where's the detergent?" Tyler opened the cabinet beneath the sink and began to arrange the assortment of bottles and boxes into some semblance of order. Something in his manner told Lacey that he just naturally tried to organize everything and everybody he touched. "Do you want to wash, Lacey, or dry?"

"Tyler, let's talk. What makes you think that just because your kisses are—"

He was running hot water into the sink as though she weren't even there.

"Are what, darling? Come on, you're one of the artistic Wilcoxes. I know what your kisses are. They're the joy of the first crocus in the spring," he warbled using the goblet he was rinsing as a microphone. "They're the softness of a child's sweet good-night kiss. They're— Ahh, I'm not a poet.

And I know, you don't have to tell me, I can't sing either."

He turned to the stack of dishes and began to separate them neatly, glasses in the dish water, plates stacked to be washed, and the silverware all sorted: spoons together, forks together, and knives resting against the side of a cooking pot. She was willing to bet that never in the history of Harmony Hall had dishes been organized and washed quite so properly. A master of quality control versus classic Wilcox haphazard hurry-up was what she was witnessing.

Crocus in the spring? A baby's good-night kiss? She couldn't quite get a handle on what Tyler was saying. She'd assumed that the reason he'd been so cool to her on the one occasion they'd met years ago, was because he so vehemently disapproved of her appearance and lifestyle. At the time he'd seemed like some kind of ice king, staring at her with cold dark eyes and maintaining an obvious distance between them.

Yet ever since she'd taken his hand and he'd pulled her close to him at the wedding, it was as if Tyler had undergone a metamorphosis, and except for the determined organization he was applying to his dishwashing, he seemed very different. And Lacey was beginning to like the man.

"I know my kisses are arresting, but do they take your voice away, Lacey?"

"Sorry, Tyler, I may be a Wilcox, but I'm not an artist. I can't be casual about personal feelings and I'm not creative; that's my mother. I . . . I—" She added in a rush, as if she realized that she'd gone too far, "I can wash these dishes by myself."

"Of course you can, but isn't it more fun if I

help?" He wadded up a dishtowel and threw it to her before turning to the stack of plates with a seriousness that took all his concentration for the next few minutes.

"Well?" He'd filled the drain board with sparkling clean glasses lined up in neat, precise rows. "Are you going to dry these dishes, or do I have to call one of the other artists in residence?"

"I'll dry," she agreed quickly. The thought of allowing Phillip, the jewelry designer, or Spence, the tap dancer, in the kitchen with Tyler was more than Lacey could envision.

What she wanted to do, she told herself, was take the towel, wrap it around his neck, and string him up from the nearest porch beam. No, what she wanted to do was use it as a whip and turn him away from the sink and into her arms. Even from a distance she was achingly aware of the feel of him where they'd touched. She'd cared for a few men, but none had torn past her reserve and invaded her feelings with such ease.

The sound of Arthur's flute drifted wistfully through the silence. She didn't recognize the tune, but she recognized the loneliness it signified. She was well acquainted with the feeling. Now and then, Tyler used a bronzed forearm to brush back the errant shock of dark hair that fell across his forehead. Lacey felt as though she were being hypnotized as she observed his small movements.

"Why are you really here, Tyler?"

She could see the muscles in his neck tighten.

"I told you," he answered in a low voice. "I came up to see your folks about the house."

"Why all the foolishness, then?"

"If you remember, I told you I tried very hard to

find out where you were after the wedding. But Mr. Carmichael didn't know your address, and outside of all those poor people named Wilcox who I badgered over the phone, I didn't know who else to ask," he explained patiently.

"I'd like to believe you, Tyler. But I have to think that your pursuit of me might have been tied into buying this house all along."

"I give you my word, I had no idea that Lacey Lee was a resident of Harmony Hall, or it wouldn't have taken me three days to find you. Why are you so suspicious, sweetheart? Do you think I go around kissing all my clients?"

She thought about what he'd said. No, she didn't think Tyler would use seduction as a ploy to buy real estate. In all honesty, she believed him when he said he didn't know her name was really Wilcox. After all, her friends always called her Lacey Lee, and the subject of her last name had never come up in her first two encounters with Tyler. But then again, what did she know? Her experience with sophisticated men was woefully limited.

Tyler's motions stopped for a moment, and she could see the tension in the set of his shoulders. "Can't you believe I'm more interested in you than in Harmony Hall?"

"I don't know."

"I've told you I adore you. All right." He threw up his hand. "I'll be serious. When I walked into the Carmichael house, the last thing I had on my mind was you, Lacey Lee. Truthfully, Callie had mentioned that you would be there, but I was so tired of hearing about how nice you were, I almost didn't go."

"So, what changed your opinion of me?"

"I'm still trying to figure that out. The minute I walked into the room and saw you, I was lost."

"Funny, you didn't look lost. I thought that Mr. Rhett Butler himself was at the wedding, charming every woman in the room. I saw you making the rounds."

"You saw me searching for you. After one quick glimpse you disappeared. If it hadn't been for Callie and Matt—"

"Yes, I'm going to have to have a little talk with Callie when she gets back. I think she must have planned all this."

"Maybe, but I'm my own man, Lacey Lee Wilcox. I make my own decisions, and when I see something I want, I go for it."

"Which brings us back to the original question, why on earth would you want me?"

"You're kind and loyal—"

"And I'm good to old people and stray animals. Please!"

". . . and tough and singleminded. You don't judge your family and you put their welfare above your own. Loyalty is a commodity in pretty short supply in today's world. I like you very much, Lacey. I haven't lied to you or your parents about that. I admire your mother and father for their open affection and honesty with each other."

"I never thought about it before. No, I guess they don't hide their feelings. Neither do I. I'm just new at this," Lacey said after a long minute. "All right. I'll admit your kisses are stimulating."

"Well, it's a start, anyway. Now, I want to know about you. Tell me about your lack of artistic ability. I mean, what do you call designing and creating dolls and clowns?"

"Making a living. Earning money. My hobby, I guess, my job. But art? No, everybody else in the family got the talent. I'm just a good seamstress."

"From what I saw in that van, you sew pretty well. How'd you begin making dolls?"

"Well, you remember that Callie and I were roommates after you were, I mean after . . ."

"After we were divorced. It's all right to talk about it. It was so long ago, I feel as if it happened in another life. Yes, I remember that you and Callie lived together in a garage apartment downtown before Callie moved to her grandfather's place up in the mountains."

"Yes, back then I was a file clerk in a dreary little insurance company, and Callie worked at a florist shop on Peachtree Street. You know the arts and crafts show they hold every year in Piedmont Park?"

"Sure, everybody knows about the Piedmont Park Art Festival."

"Well, Callie and one of her Indian friends led a protest over the lack of minorities participating in the festival, and her friend finally got permission to operate a booth. Then he got sick and ended up in the hospital. Rather than have him lose his spot, Callie and I decided to operate it for him. She made baskets and I made clowns. Lacey's Lovies."

"And Lacey's Lovies are wonderful. I bet they're the source of most of your contributions to Harmony Hall's upkeep."

"What do you know about my contributions?"

"Not much, but from what I can see of your folk's artists' colony, it may be a nice idea, but it isn't terribly successful, is it?"

"No, I'm afraid not. All the artists are still struggling, and they don't have much to contribute to a common cause."

"And if it weren't for you, this place would go down the tube, wouldn't it?"

"What exactly did Mother tell you?" Lacey felt a surge of anger at her mother. She didn't know why, but she resented her parents discussing her with an outsider. As long as they all pretended she simply dropped by occasionally, she would pretend she supported Harmony Hall voluntarily. It helped her stem the underlying feeling of bitterness toward her family.

"Nothing. It's just pretty obvious that you're the only one with both feet on the ground. This place must be a real problem to maintain."

"Unfortunately, you're right. And, as you can see, I—we're not able to do a very good job of it. I may be forced to sell my Lovies to some big toy manufacturer. You know, like the Cabbage Patch doll?"

"Oh, you can't do that, Lacey. It would be like selling a part of yourself. Besides, what about the van? You'd have to paint over Lacey's Lovies. What a crime!"

"It would be hard," she admitted, "but I have to consider the good I could do with the money. It isn't just my folks. There are others who would be hurt if Harmoney Hall isn't kept up."

The conversation seemed to have reversed direction. Tyler had gone from saying ridiculous things about his feelings for her to arguing for keeping Harmony Hall just as it was, instead of extolling the merits of selling it to him.

"Others?" he pressed, looking over his shoulder at her. "How so?"

"Oh, it's not important. Let's change the subject."

Lacey took a clean towel and finished the last of the dishes in silence as she turned the idea of selling her clowns over and over in her mind.

What would the ladies she had making clowns on consignment in their homes do if she sold her design? They needed the income. And the dolls were hers. Each one had its own personality, each one was special. Would a large company be able to continue to give those dolls that something special?

Tyler wiped off the counters and rinsed out the wash cloth. He laid it across the faucet then took Lacey's drying cloth and spread it over the wooden spokes of the towel rack.

"How did you come up with the idea for the dolls, the HuggieBabies?" he asked.

"My Lovies were first. The HuggieBabies came later. After the Cabbage Patch Kids became so successful I began to work with soft dolls. I found that I have a talent for making my dolls look like their owners. Children love them."

"That's why I said you have talent. There's all kinds of talent, Lacey. I bet that for every doll you sell, you give one away, don't you?"

Lacey nodded. Tyler had guessed what nobody else knew. She was a sucker for a kid, and she'd been to every shantytown in northern Georgia with her van. It was her own private way of saying thank you for whatever degree of success she enjoyed. She took hundreds of dolls to craft shops and festivals, but nobody knew except her how many of them she gave away.

Tyler switched off the overhead light. When he

held out his hand this time, Lacey didn't hesitate. "From the tips of your fingers," he murmured, kissing the ends of her fingers, taking each of them into his mouth as though he were tasting a fine wine, "to the tips of your toes, Lacey Lee, you're a very special lady."

"Lacey? Tyler?"

Gynneth's voice spilled across the darkness, and Lacey jerked away from Tyler like a schoolgirl caught in an embrace with her beau. She quickly switched the light on. Her mother stood in the doorway.

"Ah, yes, Mrs. Wilcox, we're just finishing in here," Tyler said smoothly. He took one last suggestive nibble on Lacey's middle finger.

Gynneth was smiling sweetly at them. "We're going up to bed now, and we wanted to say good night. We hope to see you again, Tyler."

"Oh, I think you can count on it," Tyler answered with a broad smile. "One way or another. Good night."

Lacey leaned forward to accept her mother's kiss. Gynneth hesitated for a moment, then impulsively gave Tyler a light kiss on the cheek before she glided out of the kitchen, humming, with Lacey and Tyler following. As she retreated up the dark stairwell she said, "Oh, Lacey, I have to go into town in the morning. The Daughters of the American Revolution are meeting at the Women's Club. Do you think you could prepare lunch for our guests?"

"Sure, Mother," Lacey murmured, silently calculating how much work would be involved. She was certain that she'd have to make a trip to the

grocery store first. "Would you see about the telephone while you're in town?"

"Telephone?" Gynneth repeated absently. "Yes,
I suppose I could drop by the telephone company
office. Maybe," she suggested hopefully, "it would
be easier if you talked to them, Lacey. They were
so very rude the last time I tried, and I'm afraid I
quite forgot my manners and told them I simply
would not tolerate such treatment. I just can't
deal with them personally until they apologize.
You do understand, don't you, Tyler? I mean there
comes a time when one has to be firm with people."

Lacey looked up at Tyler and found him smiling. She shrugged. He patted her shoulder.

"Wait a minute, Mother. Am I to understand
that you told Southern Bell that they were rude
and you wouldn't have anything else to do with
them until they apologized?"

"Yes, darling. That snippy little girl cut off the
phone. Can you believe such spite? Well, she isn't
going to get the best of Gynneth Lee Wilcox. I can
live without them easier than they can live without my business. Why, we, my artists and I, were
one of their best customers."

Gynneth disappeared up the stairs. After a moment, Lacey heard the soft, genteel click of her
mother's bedroom door.

"What your mother said about the phone, does
that translate the way I think it does?" Tyler asked
with smothered amusement as they walked down
the drive toward the thicket of trees where Lacey's
van was parked.

"I don't know, but I'm going to guess that Mother's guests put in a few calls to places like Tasmania and Guatemala, which caused a huge phone bill that Mother probably couldn't pay."

"And when the phone company inquired about reimbursement, Gynneth refused payment until they apologized for their bad manners."

"More than likely," Lacey agreed in embarrassment.

"They never should have been so rude to your mother. Now how am I going to call you? I'd planned to hold an intimate conversation with you while lying in my bed late tonight."

"Well, you can't. No intimate conversations. I don't know how to carry on an intimate conversation." For a moment the picture of Tyler in bed whispering into the phone was much too vivid, and she searched her mind for a safe way to change the subject.

"I'm really sorry about leaving you in the hospital the way I did, Tyler. I have your clothes in the van." Lacey was acutely conscious of the darkness and the fact that they were alone. Even Beowulf and Miranda seemed to have deserted the yard.

Their arms touched as they walked. Somewhere in the woods a whippoorwill's cry pierced the night, and Tyler jumped.

"What's wrong?" Lacey asked.

"Nothing," Tyler answered, opening the sliding door of the van, "except that I'm afraid of the dark. Will you hold my hand?"

He said it so seriously that it took a moment for her to realize he was teasing. "I could call Beowulf and Miranda to protect you."

"No, thanks, they aren't exactly the company I had in mind. I know! We could crawl inside the van and neck. Isn't necking a part of old-fashioned courting?" He sat down on the floor of the van and caught her hand.

"I wouldn't know. I'm not an old-fashioned girl."

"Oh, I think you are, Lacey Lee Wilcox. I think you're a very old-fashioned girl, and I'm beginning to like that quality in you very much."

He held her hands snugly, tracing his thumb in circles around her palm. Lacey searched for something to say to break the steadily building tension. "It's getting late. Are you sure you don't want to accept Mother's invitation to share Arthur's bedroom? I'm sure he'd lend you some pajamas."

"Lacey, I don't sleep in pajamas and it isn't *Arthur's* bed I want to share."

"Oh!" Her effort to change the conversation certainly hadn't broken the tension.

"I don't normally sleep in anything at all."

Lacey caught her breath. Tyler was sitting in her van swinging his legs over the edge of the open door. This was the van she slept in when she was on the road. She considered how she dressed when she slept, wearing oversized T-shirts or shortie pajamas. So Tyler wore nothing at all. The mental image she'd formed of him was absolutely bewitching.

"Come closer, Lacey Lee."

"No . . . no way," she stuttered. "I'm not getting in that van with you."

"Ah, come on, Lacey, let's snuggle for a minute. Pretend we're in high school and we're going to be naughty. I believe it was called smooching or some such word in your parents' time."

"Yes, but it's called foreplay now, and I'm"—her

voice dropped—"not taking any chances with you."
She looked down at their clasped hands in the
darkness. His thumb could have been touching
her all over, the way it made her body shiver.

"All right," he said softly, "just a good night
kiss, then I'll go away."

Tyler turned her hand palm up and planted a
kiss in its center, then brought it to his cheek,
rubbing it gently against the soft stubble of beard
there. He tried not to think of why he'd been sent
to Harmony Hall and what his mission would mean
to her. He tried to close out images of Lacey's big
blue eyes, knowing that if he could see them they
would be open wide in surprise. Would those big
eyes fill with hatred once she knew what he'd
been sent to do to her family?

Tyler sighed. It would have been smarter to have
remained aloof. He couldn't care about Lacey without assuming responsibility for her. That was his
way. If he allowed himself to love her, he would be
forced to love everything and everyone she cared
about, including Harmony Hall and its ne'er-do-
well inhabitants. In the darkness he heard Lacey's
swift, rough breathing. She sat down beside him,
making certain their bodies didn't touch.

"Tyler . . ."

"Shhh." He leaned over and kissed her, his
mouth touching lips that flickered in wary sur-
render, lips that parted reluctantly at first, then
for a brief moment returned his kiss before pulling away. Who was he kidding? His feelings for
Lacey had crystalized when he'd kissed her on her
front porch.

"No! No more kisses, Tyler. You're destroying
me with kisses," she whispered raggedly.

"Ah, well." He released her reluctantly. "What a way to go. Good night, Lacey Lee."

"Good night? You're actually leaving?"

"I'd rather not, darling, but after all, technically this is only our first date."

"This isn't a date, Tyler. A date is when you get dressed up and go somewhere, and don't call me darling."

"Fine, tomorrow night we go on a date. I'll pick you up at seven and we'll go out to dinner and . . ." Tyler continued, smiling, "Well, we'll just improvise the rest."

"What you'd better figure out is something else to do, because I'm turning you down, Tyler Winter. No date, no dinner. I have to work tomorrow. Good night, Tyler. It's been . . . interesting."

Before he could protest, Lacey got up and ran toward the house. As she climbed the porch steps, she had the distinct feeling that he was watching her intently. Back in the safety of her room, she heard the purr of his car's engine as he drove away. Lacey lay in bed wide eyed and wired, trying to slow her rapid breathing and the staccato beat of her heart. The lingering smell of roses in the night air wafting through her windows teased her nostrils. The lingering sensation of Tyler's touch wrapped around her body and caused a sweet ache that refused to go away.

She punched her pillow and wished that Arthur played the drums or the accordion—anything but the flute—as the melody of a bittersweet love song broke the silence of the night. Sometime before dawn she faced reality and admitted what she really wished was that she weren't so inexperienced—and Tyler Winter weren't quite such an honorable man. Being kissed good night in the darkness had been sheer, unadulterated temptation.

She'd never brought a fellow home to meet her unorthodox parents—she'd never dared. She'd never had a steady boyfriend, and she'd never been courted either. And she'd certainly never run into a man like Tyler Winter, a man who seemed determined to help her make up for lost time. Maybe she'd been hasty in refusing his dinner invitation. Maybe being courted wasn't such a bad idea.

Maybe she *was* the one who'd gotten the lick on the head.

Five

Lacey tried to put Tyler Winter out of her mind. The last thing she needed in her life was a preppy executive who lined up the silverware on the kitchen sink and still checked on his ex-wife five years after their divorce. She must have been absolutely crazy to allow him to kiss her, and to kiss him in return.

With that issue resolved, Lacey turned her attention to finding her mother's latest place for hiding bills. She discovered a telephone bill, which was two months past due, and the calls weren't to Tasmania, they were to Bora Bora. There was a plea from the local music store addressed to Arthur and a bill for repair of the hot water heater for $79.95. Lacey took the bill and went in search of explanations.

"Mother? Mother! Daddy, do you have any idea where Mother is?"

"I believe she's gone into town," Alfred Wilcox said, looking up from a sheaf of papers he was reading in the library. "Is there anything I can tell you?"

"Daddy, why do we have a bill for hot water heater repairs of $79.95?"

"Wasn't it wonderful? Your mother was able to find someone to repair our old one. Saved us the cost of a new heater, didn't she?"

"Except that if the shower I took last night is any indication, it isn't fixed."

When the phone rang Lacey almost didn't hear it, between Spence's stereo booming and Arthur's drums. Arthur had started on bagpipes this morning and progressed to drums. Mr. Spragg was hammering away in the barn, and Spence was rehearsing a new arrangement of the *The Music Man* with a double tap accompaniment. No wonder her mother disappeared regularly. She couldn't understand how her father stood the din until she caught sight of the wads of cotton in his ears. Lacey put a finger to one ear and held the phone to the other.

"Hello?"

"Good morning, darling. I see the phone is working."

It was Tyler. Lacey covered her surprise with a gruff response. "Yes, Mother went to town and made friends with Ma Bell. What do you want?"

"You."

His answer was direct and didn't help her mood at all. In fact, just hearing his voice contributed to her confused state of mind. Even her mother's wacky measures to save money were beginning to make sense.

"Don't do this to me, Tyler. This isn't *Fantasy Island.* Fun and games are over."

"Darn! And I had such fun games planned for lunch."

"Don't you have work to do, Tyler?"

"Nothing I can't delegate."

"Well, I'm not an executive. I have to do my work myself."

"I'll help you."

"No, thanks. Unless you're into counterfeiting money, I don't think even you can untangle things. Mother has practiced what you might call creative bookkeeping." Lacey stopped, guilty over her anger. Her family's financial problems weren't his fault. "I'm sorry, Tyler, I just don't have time for you in my life, charming though you may be."

"I see. Are we having our first fight?"

"Tyler, we're not fighting, we're finishing. Please, I've spent the morning finding all the letters and bills Mother had hidden away, and I'm not in any mood to fence with you."

"Letters?" Tyler felt a sense of panic run through him. His pulse began to pound and his heart dropped down to his sock tops. She'd find out about the past-due mortgage payments and know what business he really had at Harmony Hall before he could explain.

"Yes, letters," she answered wearily. "I don't know how I'm going to manage, but I will. I always have. Oh, hell, why am I telling you all this?"

Hearing the anguish in her voice, Tyler wanted to throw down the phone and fly to her side, take her in his arms and tell her he'd fix everything—but he couldn't. She wasn't ready to let him—not yet. That he'd stopped by the telephone company and had the phone reconnected was a fact he'd keep to himself. Given Gynneth's eccentricity, he doubted Lacey would ever suspect he'd been the one to pacify—and pay—Ma Bell.

"I know what you're going through, Lacey. You may not believe it, but I really do understand. Someday I'll tell you about my family. Please know that you can talk to me. What are friends for, if not to share their troubles?"

"Friends?" Lacey's voice was weary. "I don't think of us as friends."

"That's where you're wrong, Lacey. Friends are people who know your darkest secrets and your deepest fears, and love you anyway."

"And what makes you think that you qualify in that department?"

"Oh, I definitely do. For instance, I know that you share your bed with a duck, and I haven't told a soul."

She couldn't help laughing. "Oh, Tyler, you nut."

"Friend," he corrected with a warm chuckle. "That's me, kid, and a friend is there when you need him. I'll be over in half an hour. You forget your worries, and I'll put on a show that'll make you laugh, I promise."

"A show? Are you a closet performer?" Lacey couldn't help but respond to Tyler. He had a way of reducing her worst fear to a mere inconvenience.

"No, but you may think I belong in a closet when you see me in my jams."

"Your what?"

"Jams. You just wait, darling. Today you're going to meet the fun-seeking Tyler Winter. Sit tight. If my jams don't put that lovely smile back on your face, you're hopeless."

"Oh, Tyler, you're crazy. I'm already smiling and

I can't wait to see what jams are." Lacey rubbed her temple, gauging the tendrils of discomfort that promised to become a headache.

"Good enough. I'll be there shortly."

Lacey put away her household accounts and laid out the lunch fixings. She changed into a soft, peach-colored sundress and delegated the preparation of lunch to Spence, who was tapping away at the counter when Lacey went out the front door and down the drive. She picked her way through the weeds past the vine-covered swimming pool, with its cracked tiles and sad look of neglect.

Lacey glanced around at the overgrown yard and the outbuildings that begged for fresh paint, and she sniffed the sweet odor of the honeysuckle blossoms. Was it foolish to disregard Tyler's offer to buy Harmony Hall? she wondered.

The honeysuckle partially covered the evidence of the pool's disrepair and it did smell so sweet. Though overgrown, the vine had redeeming value, like her home. Maybe the house and barn could be held and the rest of the land sold. Lacey sighed. No, the land had belonged to the Wilcox family since before the Civil War. If her great-grandfather had managed to hold on to it, so could she. She'd just have to redouble her efforts. More dolls. More craft shows. She wandered back past the pool to the gazebo and propped herself on the rail, wondering what the grounds must have looked like in the time of her famous ancestor, General Robert E. Lee. After Sherman rearranged the landscape, times had been hard. If it hadn't been for General Lee and some well-placed family friends, Harmony Hall would never have been rebuilt. Too bad she didn't have some well-placed friends to come to the rescue now.

"Hello, gypsy. Where's my smile?"

"Oh, Tyler. It didn't take you long." Lacey turned to face him, trying to keep the eagerness from her voice. She let her gaze range over him and tried desperately not to laugh out loud at what she saw. He was tromping through the weeds carrying a picnic basket and wearing the lavender clown T-shirt she'd bought him. It clashed with the weirdest shorts she'd ever seen: pink flamingos against a blue background with bright yellow flowers. All he needed was a pair of oversized shoes and he'd make a perfect Bozo.

"I had one foot on the gas pedal when I called. What do you think? Worth waiting for?" He stretched his arms and turned around slowly, exhibiting himself like a music box figure.

"I'm impressed. The . . . whatever those things are, are awesome. I don't believe I've ever seen anything quite like them. And you're the only man in the world who could wear them and still look appealing."

"That's what my loyal secretary said when I came to work this morning. I gave her the afternoon off, in gratitude."

"You went to work dressed like that?"

"No, I just went in to tell my assistant that you and I are going on a picnic, and tomorrow we're going to an art exhibit. Now, for the picnic."

"We're going to have a picnic? Here?"

"Why not? It's private. I gave orders that we weren't to be disturbed. Help me spread out this blanket. We'll cover up the dirt on the floor and let the games begin."

She managed to pull her gaze away from Tyler's jams to noticed the old army blanket he had in his hands. They spread the blanket across the gazebo's aging wood floor, then Tyler sat down and opened the picnic basket.

'Well, are you going to eat standing up?" he asked.

Lacey looked around the gazebo and back down at the man dressed in the outlandish outfit. "I don't believe this."

"I know, but you will. Which do you prefer, ham and swiss on rye, chicken salad, or roast beef with horseradish?"

She dropped to the blanket beside him. The man was impossible He was a chameleon, taking on the look and personality of his surroundings. From the polished, calendar-hunk of an executive she'd met at the wedding, he'd turned into Moon Doggie, the beach bum.

"You don't have anything against regular food, do you?" Tyler inquired patiently.

"I'll take the roast beef with horseradish."

"Aha! I knew you'd pick the spicy food. That's my Lacey. She prefers the simple, standard old roast beef—but laced with spice."

"Horsefeathers!" Lacey stated.

"No, it's horseradish, and I've already sampled its fire. Come here, darling." He gave her a warm smile, caught her wrist, and pulled her close. "You look much too serious." When he began to tickle her ribs, Lacey squealed and tried to slide out of his reach.

"How . . . how dare you, Tyler!" She gulped between giggles, trying desperately to get away, but then he was beside her on the blanket, leaning over her, that errant shaft of dark hair falling over his left brow. She finally gave in to the urge she'd been fighting since the wedding. She reached up and threaded her fingers through his hair's rich, warm softness, pushing it back into place.

He sighed. "Ah, Lacey. Just look at what's happening to us. I'm wearing pink flamingo pants, and you're laying here, touching me, just asking to be kissed."

"But I'm not," she began. "I don't want you to kiss me anymore, Tyler. I don't want you to invite me on picnics, and I certainly don't want to be courted. We don't have anything in common. Oh, Tyler, just be my friend."

"It's already gone past friendship, Lacey. And I want to court you. You're a lady who deserves to be cherished. You've spent all your life doing for other people. You need someone to do for you. I think the someone you need is me."

Tyler studied her thoughtfully. The wistful way she'd said "just be my friend" provoked every protective and loving urge in his soul. He couldn't believe what was going on inside him, all the turmoil and contradiction. He wanted to hold her tenderly in his arms and take care of her. He wanted to ravish her, carry her off to his castle in the sky and make mad, passionate love to her forever.

"Tyler? Tyler, are you all right?"

He shook his head, trying to clear it. No, he wasn't all right. He definitely wasn't all right. Here he was in the middle of the day, dressed in the only outlandish outfit he'd ever owned, on the floor of a dilapidated old gazebo, with his arms around a carrot-haired girl with fire in her eyes.

"Lacey"—his voice dropped—"let's pretend that we're trapped in the castle of an evil sorcerer. We're alone. The evil sorcerer's evil guards are coming soon to take me to the dungeon. I'll be executed at dawn, and kissing you is my last wish."

He was doing it again, drawing her into his spell. She stared groggily into his warm brown eyes, which were dancing now with merriment. "Executed? At dawn?"

"Lacey, you're so beautiful. Kiss me once before the guards arrive."

"Me? Beautiful? Now I know you're sick."

The confusion on her face was genuine. She knew that he desired her. She wanted him as well. But she'd never deceived herself. "Oh, Tyler, let's not get carried away. You told me yourself that you always get what you want. I don't want to be another conquest. You're a sophisticated, handsome man. I'm a red-haired flake. But beautiful? That, I'm not."

"Lacey, darling, take a good look at me. Beauty is in the eyes of the beholder. Would anybody in the world except you and my bonus-conscious secretary say that I'm appealing today?"

"Probably not," she agreed with a smile. "But I love the jams, particularly the pink flamingos."

"And I love the way you look. You hair is fire from the sun, your eyes sparkle like rare jewels, and your lips— There's no describing your lips, darling. I'm just going to have to show you."

Lacey's eyelids closed and her lips parted. His mouth was sweet and he kissed her gently, a long, lingering kiss that warmed her and told her more surely than words that he, too, was caught up in the fantasy of the gazebo.

He pulled away and lifted her to a sitting position. Lacey leaned heavily against him, her head on his shoulder. "Now, m'lady," he whispered, "I want to know more about you. Let's start with something innocent. What's your favorite color?"

She thought for a moment, unable to remember. "Red,"—her voice was breathless—"but I can't wear it. Do you have something to drink? I'm . . . I'm awfully warm."

He chuckled. "Certainly. We are on a picnic. I have lemonade."

An hour later they finished lunch. She'd asked him all the whimsical things she could think of. He had a secret passion for yellow. He liked to have his back scratched and he hated spinach. He'd bought a skate board and had taken it down to the parking area of his building to try it out.

Lacey told him that she loved pizza and roasted peanuts, and that she hated to have anyone else drive her van. She confessed her passion for the Three Stooges, and he admitted a secret love for Foghorn J. Leghorn and Bugs Bunny. And every time he tried to ask a serious question, she refused to answer. It was mid-afternoon before the sun drove them from their playhouse. Lacey helped Tyler refold the blanket and gather up the trash.

"I wish you had a pool. A swim would be nice." Tyler wiped beads of perspiration from his forehead.

"We do, or we did have one. A crack started in the wall, and then the filter system went out. The pool hasn't been used in years." She led him through the tangled flower bed to the honeysuckle-covered spot near the patio. "It's over here."

Tyler looked at the pool and groaned. At some point back in the early forties, it must have been a lovely creation. Now green slime and mold filled one end, and a mixture of the vines, and poison ivy wrapped round the ceramic tile edges.

"I have a friend in the pool business," Tyler began. "We could get him to come by and repair the crack in no time."

"No, Tyler."

"And my maintenance men could clear away these vines in an afternoon. I'll bet your mother used to entertain out here. I can just see floating baskets in the pool, and we could meet out here for secret midnight swims . . ."

Midnight swims? With Tyler? Her heart seemed to plunge to her knees. "Tyler! Please! I think you'd better go. I have to see about dinner."

"Lacey." He took a step toward her. His hands moved to her shoulders and dug into her skin in pure frustration. "Lacey. Let me help you. You could consider it a loan—pay me when you can."

"No. No, Tyler. Don't. I can't accept your help. I couldn't pay you back. It's all I can do to—" she raised her eyes, choking back a sob. "Damn, why do I care about a silly old pool with a crack in it? Why don't I let your company buy this place and move my folks somewhere comfortable?"

"Because you love it," he answered simply, and cradled her head against his shoulder, touching his lips to her temple. "Your family needs you and you're there for them. They're like your children— they claim all of you." There was a soothing sadness in his touch, and she felt tears well up in her eyes and spill over in a cleansing stream of release.

And they don't leave much for me, he thought as he held her. Gradually she relaxed and leaned against him, allowing him to comfort her. The tough facade fell away, and he was glad that she'd let him get close to her. He had to tell her the truth. She had to know that she had a much bigger problem with Harmony Hall than the pool.

"Lacey," he said finally. "There's something I have to tell you. I'm a fraud."

"I know."

"Lacey, I'm trying to be serious." She pulled away and smiled up at him.

"So am I. You're not really a beach bum. You've been found out." She laughed lightly and spun away, the moment for seriousness past.

He gave up. He'd tell her later. She's just gotten through a bad moment. No point in bringing the pain back. "So jams aren't my regular attire. How can you tell?"

"The price tag is still on them. I can't believe you paid thirty-nine dollars for those. Give me thirty-nine dollars and about an hour, and we could stitch up two dozen pairs of those pants. Speaking of which, I have to get back to work." She kissed him lightly on the cheek. He tasted of lemonade and salt. "Good-bye. Thanks for a lovely afternoon."

"You're making me go?"

"I'm making you go."

"How about dinner tonight?"

"No."

"Tomorrow night?"

"No."

"I'll call you," he said with authority. "We're still going to the art exhibit tomorrow."

"Maybe. I might not be here when you call."

"I'll find you." He raised a warning finger. "I'll always find you, Lacey." He took her face between his hands and kissed her thoroughly. "I know what you want. I know what you need," he whispered against her lips. Then he let go of her, winked, and walked toward his car. The happy, flushed look he left on her face gave him a quiet sense of victory.

It was ironic, Tyler thought as he drive back to his condo in northern Atlanta. Twice in his life he'd found women he could care about and both times they were gypsy women with fire in their veins and the call of the open road in their souls. Callie had been a free spirit. He'd tried to tame her, and he'd lost her.

And now there was Lacey—feisty, proud, independent Lacey—who took people under her wing and cared for them. She'd looked after him at her friend's wedding, and she paid her parents' bills and solved their problems with a fierce protectiveness he could appreciate. She was fighting a losing battle in her efforts to keep Harmony Hall afloat, and he didn't know how he was going to be able to tell her that he was the enemy.

When he reached his condo, Tyler drove his car into his private space in the underground garage. Concrete and steel and insulated elegance, he thought, as the elevator carried him silently to the penthouse suite. His house was like his life— sterile. It was nothing like the gazebo with its peeling paint, or like Harmony Hall's front porch swing with the bright yellow cushions. Nothing, he concluded, like the loving atmosphere of Lacey's home. Genteel, impoverished artists? Yes, every one. But there was something special about those people and that proud old house, something that had to be preserved.

"They usually keep the most popular works on display in this room." Tyler guided Lacey down the dim corridor and into a room dotted with small shelves and special spotlights. "I think you'll find this display particularly interesting."

"Come here often, do you?" Lacey smothered a giggle and tried to look serious as she examined what appeared to be clay-coated sex organs that had beady eyes in strange places.

"Not recently," Tyler answered, viewing the display with alarm. "When I called, the director said the gallery was featuring a fantasy collection, and I thought it might be something that a lady who made Lovies might like."

Truthfully, he realized, the last time he'd been there was over a year ago, when he'd spied an unusual display in the window. He and the owner had shared a pleasant afternoon discussing abstract art and the public's acceptance or lack of acceptance of it. Tyler looked around uneasily. This display left much to be desired.

The art gallery was almost empty. Only one rather furtive, pale-skinned boy, with an earring in one ear and bare feet, shared the long silent room with them. After he caught the boy sending several secretive grins at Lacey, Tyler pulled her into the next room.

"Ah, this is much better. These are some of Alton Kersey's new works. Alton and I were in school together way back when."

Lacey glanced curiously at the large colorful

canvases. While not particularly knowledgeable about abstract art, Lacey could feel a sense of power in the paintings. She listened carefully as Tyler exhibited a sizable degree of expertise in explaining the concepts.

"You really do know about art, don't you?"

"Of course I do. I was an art major, and not commercial art, Lacey, love. I once had visions of becoming another Salvador Dali."

"What really stopped you?"

Tyler's expression turned serious. He leaned forward and twirled his fingers imaginatively. "I couldn't grow the mustache."

"Be serious, Tyler. Don't you paint at all?"

"Not anymore. I stopped a long time ago. But" —he grinned and lifted his head as if he were in deep thought—"after seeing that display in the other room, I might consider taking up working with clay. What do you think?"

"I think you miss art, Tyler Winter, and I think that somehow you've gotten me and my family confused with the world you left behind. Don't do it. You aren't the same person now that you were then. And I'm not Callie."

They looked at each other for a long moment before Tyler replied.

"No, you're not Callie. The past is past, Lacey Lee Wilcox. You're the now." Tyler took her hands and studied them, drawing her to him.

"Don't, Tyler, don't expect more from me than I can give," Lacey pleaded, her blue eyes swimming with unshed tears. "I'm sorry."

He probed the depths of her eyes, searching for words to express what he wanted to say. "Don't ever be sorry, Lacey Lee. You're sunshine and happiness. You're picnics and clowns. You've brought a joy to my life that's been missing, and I never even knew it until now."

"Me?" she questioned.

"You, and I'm having a very hard time controlling the urge to skip pretending to be artistic and jump straight to being passionate. I think the clay display got to me. What do you say? Did you get any inspiration?"

"Oh, my goodness," Lacey said with a laugh, "I've met the romantic Tyler, the fun-loving Tyler, and the artistic Tyler. The only Tyler I'm interested in meeting right now, however, is the hungry one. Do you suppose we could find an ice cream stand?"

Tyler laughed and flung his arm across his forehead in mock dismay. "You mean you'd pass up passion for pistachio? I'm crushed. So much for art, woman. Let's find a nice quiet place and smother each other with whipped cream and cherries. I suddenly feel very creative."

He had been fun and creative, and Lacey laughed more than she had in years. And between bites of ice cream he only kissed her twice. When he took her home he brushed her cheek with his lips and said good night. There'd been no pressure to go further, she'd found it more disturbing than she'd admit, even to herself. Every time he came around, more of barriers of her life came tumbling down.

Six

"Mother, I wish you'd keep all the bills in the same place instead of leaving them scattered all over. How on earth can I be sure they're all here?"

"Bills? Oh, yes. That's right," Gynneth offered. She lay on her satin-covered bed, enjoying a facial made of cucumbers. A slice of cucumber covered each eye. "I moved the household accounts into your father's office. You found them, didn't you?"

"Finally. At least I think I did. I wish you'd take those green things off your eyes. You look like Kermit the Frog."

"Are you cross, darling? Did you have a spat with your young man?"

"He's not my young man."

"Now, Lacey. When a Wilcox woman meets the right man, she knows. Stop being so uptight. Let yourself be happy, Lacey darling. You deserve it. I've been so worried about you ever finding a man that would make you as happy as I've been."

Lacey forced a smile and leaned over to kiss her

mother. "Don't worry, Mother. It'll work out. Maybe I'll try those cucumbers, if they'll keep me looking as young as you."

"Oh, sweetie. I forgot to tell you. Tyler called to remind you that he's taking you to dinner tonight. He said he'd be here at six o'clock."

Lacey stopped. "But, Mother, we don't have a date for dinner. I told Tyler that I wasn't going out with him."

"Oh? Well I think you're wrong. He'll be here. Tyler Winter isn't a young man who takes no for an answer." Her voice softened. "Lacey, you're my daughter and I love you. I'd think twice about playing hard to get. He seems awfully nice."

"And I suppose the two of you discussed me?"

"Not really. Tyler has such lovely manners. Do you know he's sending his yard man over to clear out the pool?"

"Oh, no he isn't!" Lacey's voice rose in anger. This time he'd gone too far. The picnic was fun. The trip to the art gallery was fun. But cleaning out the pool wasn't fun. It was a bribe for her mother's approval, and Lacey wouldn't tolerate it. Her family was her responsibility, and if the pool needed work, she'd see to it.

"But, Lacey,"—Gynneth sat up and removed the cucumber slices—"I must confess, it will be wonderful to have our pool back again. I've really missed my morning swims, but if it bothers you . . ."

Lacey turned away. She couldn't miss the longing in her mother's voice. What difference did it make? she asked herself. Tyler had money, and if he wanted to spend it on their pool, well, she'd just have to sell some extra dolls to repay him. She went downstairs to the living room and spent the afternoon going over her inventory. At six o'clock her mother interrupted.

"Lacey, hadn't you better get ready for your date? Your young man will be here any minute now."

"Tyler isn't coming, Mother. I left a message on his answering machine and with his secretary. We don't have a date. I have too much work to do."

"Nonsense. What work?"

"Well, there are the bills, and I have to make arrangements to add another craft show to my list."

"Tomorrow, Lacey. Tomorrow is soon enough. It's Saturday evening, time for fun. Right now you'd better scoot upstairs and dress. Tyler will be here, I'm sure. Would you like me to peel a cucumber for your eyes?"

"Not tonight, Mother." Lacey allowed herself to be sent upstairs. She had no intention of going out to dinner, she told herself for at least five minutes. For the next five minutes she stared out the turret window into the garden, trying earnestly to erase the memory of Tyler Winter from her thoughts. Even the walls of her room seemed to have been imprinted with the aura of the man.

She shouldn't go out with him. She wouldn't go out with him. But she ought to talk with him about the pool, she decided. Oh, this was all her mother's fault. She probably orchestrated the entire evening. She and Tyler didn't need Lacey at all. Lacey groaned. "I'm so weak," she muttered, admitting that she wanted to be with Tyler Winter.

She'd get ready, just in case.

Lacey took a quick shower, then jerked open the door to her closet and surveyed the contents.

Her choices were the lavender dress she'd worn to the wedding or a skirt and blouse. Her wardrobe had degenerated in the last few years. She described it as somewhere between country casual and thrift shop mix-and-match.

Before she could decide what to wear, she heard the sound of an engine followed by the dogs' barking. He was here. Her pulse quickened.

A telltale creak outside her door announced either her mother's or Tyler's impending presence, and she was still standing before the mirror wearing only her panties. Well, anything was better than having him find her half dressed. Lacey made a mad grab at a green gauzy skirt and a long-sleeved yellow cotton shirt-jacket. She left the top three buttons open, added a longer petticoat that showed its teasing ruffle beneath her skirt, and ran a comb through her still-damp hair.

"Lacey?" It was Tyler. "Are you ready, darling?"

"Uhmmm. Just give me a minute." A touch of blusher, a smear of green eyeshadow, mascara, and a slash of coral lipstick, and she was ready —as ready as she'd ever be. No femme fatale here, she decided, and flung open the door.

"Hi!" she called out, and swallowed anything else she might have added in weak admiration. Tyler looked like he belonged in a credit card commercial. He was wearing a loose fitting pair of buff-colored trousers and a matching cotton jacket with the sleeves rolled up. His Italian loafers covered sockless feet, and his dark brown shirt was unbuttoned almost halfway down his very handsome chest.

"Lacey, you're lovely." He pushed the door open wide, and they stared at each other. When he pulled her forward, she slid her arms around his lower back and sighed her pleasure, opening her lips to his as if the encounter had been planned. He gave her a lingering, gentle kiss.

Finally she managed to whisper, "Didn't anybody ever tell you about doorbells?"

"I tried the doorbell. I don't think it works. Beowulf was the only one who seemed to know I was expected. Spence finally let me in. I think your folks want us to be alone."

"Oh. They're good at manipulating, all right." He kissed her again. "Dinner," she finally managed to say.

"I always eat my dessert first," he said gruffly, and proceeded to taste every part of her willing mouth.

Long minutes passed. He ran his hands lightly up and down her back, setting off delicious shivers in their wake. Lacey gave in to temptation and returned the languid caress on his back.

His hand eased around to stroke her right breast. Lacey gasped at the instant reaction of her nipple and the sudden realization that he was pressing an unmistakable hardness against her lower stomach. She moaned. "Oh, Tyler. What am I going to do with you?"

"Obvious suggestions aside, Lacey, I'm at the point where I'd better back away. If we don't get downstairs pretty quick, we may find out how many people actually know I'm here. Mr. Spragg may have lost his duck again."

Her heart thudding, Lacy pulled away from him and walked weakly toward the staircase, her mind jumbled with feelings that she couldn't seem to control. He was driving her crazy. He'd announced that he was coming after her, and nothing she did seemed to deter him. What was worse was that every time he came at her, all her defenses collapsed and she turned into limp spaghetti. She was practically throwing herself at him, and her mother wasn't helping the situation. No doubt she'd told Tyler to come to Lacey's bedroom. What a way for a parent to behave!

"Lacey! Wait!" Tyler leaned unsteadily against the doorframe, his eyes closed, his breath coming in deep, uneven gulps. What had he done? He'd planned to be old-fashioned and court Lacey slowly, giving her time to discover that they belonged together. It was the only way to reach her. He could seduce Lacey. Every time he held her in his arms he felt her respond, but that wasn't the right approach. She had to know that she wanted him. He had to stop kissing her. Hell, he couldn't even convince himself. All he wanted to do was jerk her back into the room and lock the door, and he guessed that her mother and father's disappearance was designed to make it possible. Gynneth wasn't the flake she appeared to be. She was a pretty smart woman.

Go slow, he told himself. "Don't run away from me. I'm not a lecherous old goat."

"At this point, I'm beginning to feel like the lecherous goat." Lacey clung to the top of the banister and turned back to look at him, her chest rising and falling spasmodically.

"Ba-a-ah. We make a good pair, then." Smiling crookedly, Tyler walked over and took her by the elbow. He directed her down the steps and past the kitchen, where her father and Spence were bent over peering intently into the oven.

"We're leaving now, sir," Tyler called.

"Fine, fine. Don't stay out too late." Alfred waved his approval and took a deep sniff of whatever was baking.

"Have a nice time," Gynneth called from the pantry.

"I hope you like what I have planned," Tyler said as they walked down the hallway and out onto the front porch.

Beowulf, lying stretched across the front step, lazily opened one eye. Miranda sprang from the sidewalk, growling and snapping at Lacey as though she'd never laid eyes on her before.

"Miranda!"

"Okay, you two devil hounds, split!" Tyler's voice left no room for disagreement, and both animals sheepishly vacated the steps.

Amazed, Lacey watched them. "I don't know why I should be surprised," she noted drolly. "The dogs, Mother, Daddy, my brother—you've hypnotized them all, haven't you? I'll bet you're a very successful real estate salesman."

"Oh, I'm not in sales. The finance and management end of the business are my line." He opened the door of his sleek foreign car and assisted Lacey inside. When he settled in the driver's seat he said, "Sometimes I think your folks have the right idea—avoid the rat-race, do your own thing on your own terms."

"Oh sure, do you want to rent Arthur's bed and become an oriental matzo-ball maker or something?"

"Maybe," he said softly. "Maybe that wouldn't be so bad, if I could inspire such loyalty in you." She looked at him incredulously. He cleared his throat. "About dinner. I thought we'd go some-place informal. I want you to relax so that we can talk seriously."

"Talk seriously?" She laughed to cover her nervousness.

"I think," Tyler said as he started the engine and put the car in gear, "that you've had enough of fun and games. You've met Tyler the romantic and Tyler the fun guy. But tonight we're down to Tyler the serious. How about a temporary truce in the fun and games. What do you think?"

"If a truce means no touching and no kissing, I'll agree."

"That's going to be very hard, but I'll try," Tyler promised solemnly.

Not any harder than it is for me, Lacey thought.

After the bargain was struck, Lacey began to relax. The night was cooler than she'd expected and she wished she'd worn a light jacket.

Tyler changed gears with graceful, expert move-ments. He didn't speak and neither did she. She pretended to watch the highway, but from the corner of her eye she was aware only of him. She might be able to keep her wits about her if she could ignore the strand of dark hair that seemed intent on sliding down over his eyebrow. Lacey stiffened as she fought the insane urge to push it back where it belonged.

By the time he parked the car in the parking lot of the State Line Barbecue and Steak Palace, Lacey had lost her appetite. She shivered. "Cold?" Tyler cut off the engine and reached for her arm.

"Hardly. I mean . . . a little. But I'll be all right once I get some hot barbecue sauce inside me. It is hot, isn't it?"

"Hot? Hell, the sauce here is hot enough to curl your toes." Tyler walked around to her door, opened it, and held out his hand.

"Fine," she said with a dare in her voice as she took his hand and stood up, her body brushing his. "But what if I'm not accustomed to having my toes curled?"

"Then, my desirable lady, I'll have to help you practice." He grinned, took her arm, and escorted her inside.

So much for truces, Lacey decided. Tyler asked for the darkest corner booth away from the sound of western music being played by a three-piece group at one end of the huge barnlike room.

"Good atmosphere for talking," she observed, raising her voice to be heard.

"I didn't think you'd go for candlelight and violins. Would you rather be closer to the band?"

She glanced around. "No. This looks like a fun place."

It was. Tyler ordered the house special, barbecued ribs, mounds of greasy fries, and cole slaw that was so vinegary Lacey's mouth prickled. Then he talked. Beginning with his high school days, he told Lacey about his family, his father who was a construction worker who usually spent his weekly paycheck before he got home on Friday night, and about his mother who simply withered away under the constant pressure of bill collectors and mental abuse until she died. After her death the state welfare authorities had come and taken Tyler to a foster home.

"Oh, Tyler," Lacey murmured. "I'm so sorry."

He shrugged. "I'm not telling you all this to get sympathy. I just want you to know my background.

After I went into the foster home, I learned how normal people live. It didn't take long for me to decide that I preferred beauty to ugliness. I guess that's why I began to paint."

"Were the foster homes bad?" Lacey's family might have been unorthodox, but they'd always been a family. She looked at Tyler and tried to imagine how it felt to be abandoned. And somehow she understood, understood that there was more than one kind of abandonment. Life could leave you behind, or you could close yourself away from life. In either case the end result was learning about loneliness first hand.

"No, not really. But they were pretty bleak. I had to make my own beauty, which I did by painting. I vowed I'd never give in to ugliness again if I could help it. That's why I decide to overrule you and send my cleaning men over to clear out the pool. I can't stand to see beautiful things or beautiful people go to ruin."

The earnest look in his eyes took away her objections. "It was a nice gesture, from a very nice person," she allowed. "My mother is thrilled. For that, I thank you."

He nodded. "What else would you like to know about me, Lacey?"

"Well. How did you and Callie meet?"

"I thought Callie had told you all about us."

"No, Callie is a very private person. All I ever knew was that you'd been married once and that you were still friends. She lumped you, her grandfather's friend John Henry and William her goat into the same category: Loveable pests."

"That's me, all right, a loveable pest."

When Tyler looked at her, the simple pleasure

in his expression was so obvious that Lacey felt her heart take a quick little beat. The more he talked the more she wanted to know. "Go on," she urged. "Tell me about Callie."

"We met at the High Museum of Art. Callie and I were both art students on a tour of the gallery. I spotted Callie immediately, but it took me one whole wall of paintings before I could ease myself out of my college's group and into hers."

"Where were you in school?"

"She was a student at Emory University—very ritzy, I'm sure you know—and I was a struggling artist working my way through Georgia State."

"You were majoring in art then? But you're in real estate now. What happened?"

A painful look flashed across his face. "I needed money."

Lacey ate in silence for a few minutes, wondering whether or not to ask the question that was nagging at her. She didn't know what Tyler had planned for the evening, but she hadn't expected him to bare his soul, nor would she have guessed that she'd be so interested in knowing about his past.

She tipped her head back and asked quietly, "Why did you and Callie really separate? She never told me, Tyler."

"I told myself it was because we just grew up, Lacey. We were too young when we married. Callie and I were both looking for someone to hold onto, an anchor, and we were happy, very happy, in the beginning. We had great dreams. We were going to save the world. But sometimes good intentions go bad, and the bad just grows and grows." He paused, and Lacey knew there was more to the story than he'd told her, more that he didn't want to talk about, and she'd respect his wish.

After a long moment he gave a sad smile and went on. "And I guess that people change, grow in different directions. Art is wonderful for the soul, but it doesn't pay the bills. And there comes a time when a person has to face reality."

"Don't I know." Lacey shook her head. "Look at my folks."

"But your folks are happy, and that's important too. Money isn't everything. Look at you, Lacey. Look at how hard you work. What do you really want for yourself?"

"Me? I don't know. I've never really thought about it. I like my life, I guess. I like creating and selling my dolls and traveling the craft show circuit. It's nice to be free from the demands of my family when I'm away. Not that I don't love them. I do. But they're a real responsibility."

"Yes, I know all about responsibility. Looking after the people I love is a bad habit of mine. I still check in on Callie, she's my friend, and Matt is too." He paused, frowning. "Damn, how'd we get onto this topic? I'm out with the woman I'm courting and I'm talking about my ex-wife." He looked around suddenly, motioning to the waitress for more iced tea.

Lacey pretended sudden interest in a basket of cornbread and muffins as she choked back an urge to slide around the red-plastic-covered booth and hug him.

"We aren't courting, Tyler. You don't have to keep up the pretense. I'm just some kind of novelty to you. The game has been fun."

"It may have started out as a joke, but being

with you just gets better and better. We're both practical, pragmatic, and passionate. What else could you ask for in a relationship?"

Unselfish love. Lacey clenched her teeth to keep from saying so out loud. Her family loved her, certainly, but that love was mixed with all sorts of needs. She provided, they accepted. Unselfish love was something she didn't know much about, and something she desperately needed. She didn't want to admit that Tyler Winter had become a part of the need.

"Now, Miss Gypsy,"—Tyler cleared his throat and gave her a stern look—"let's talk about you. Let me hear all your most intimate secrets."

"Hmmm, I'm afraid I don't have any. No past marriages, not even a broken engagement. You're probably talking to the dullest woman in north Georgia. My flamboyant sister, Medina, was the brightest female in the Wilcox galaxy."

"You mean the ballet dancer who lives with the guru in Soho?"

"How'd you know about Medina?"

"Gynneth told me. We had a nice long chat on the telephone while you were shopping. But you're wrong. Your mother is very proud of you, Lacey. She envies you your self-confidence."

"My mother is proud of me?" Lacey couldn't keep the shock from her voice. "She has an odd way of showing it."

"I didn't say she understood you, darling. But she sees how quietly and efficiently you go about your business. You never get upset, you're loyal, and you care. Lacey, I think you're just about perfect. Besides," he added with a wink, "I know that you have a secret talent that you aren't even aware of."

"I do? What?"

"Provoking men to wild fantasies," he said with a groan. "When you look at me like that, love, I want to vault across this table and grab you. Isn't that a talent? But I promised a truce, didn't I?" He sighed.

"You mean I have a talent for enticing men into dark corners?" Lacey was beginning to appreciate the fact that there was a table between them. She could relax and tease Tyler. Teasing was a skill she'd never cultivated. Maybe, she considered, she'd never cared deeply about a man before, but she was ready to admit that she cared a great deal about the man who was sitting across from her.

"Something like that," he admitted as he tossed his napkin down and pushed back the plate piled high with rib bones. He grinned at her.

"Well, you're pretty talented yourself, Tyler. You're wonderful with people. I shouldn't compliment you. No point in giving you a swelled head about it."

Tyler groaned. "Listen, my crazy lady, my head isn't the part of my body you have to worry about. Let's dance."

"Dance?" She glanced at the postage-stamp-sized dance floor across the room. "I hadn't noticed the dance floor from where we're sitting." She wasn't being totally honest. She'd noticed the dance floor right away, wondering how it would feel to dance up close, touching, with Tyler.

The western band was playing a mournful tune about unhappy love when Tyler stood up and offered his hand. Before they'd even reached the dance floor, Lacey realized that she was making a mistake. There'd be no table between them now. Tyler gathered her close, draping both arms around her back, leaving her little choice but to latch her fingers behind his neck.

"Just like the wedding," he whispered, molding himself intimately against her.

"Yes." Lacey swallowed hard, following the beat of the music.

Love is two people loving, don't try to make it more, the singer crooned. *It isn't complicated, lady, you don't have to know the score.* The words didn't make much sense, yet Lacey knew what the songwriter had been trying to say. Love was loving somebody, wanting to be close, to share pain and joy.

Then it came to her.

She felt her life shatter into a million fragments as fear pierced her body with such pain that she moaned out loud.

She understood what her mother had been trying to tell her. She understood what her body had been trying to tell her. She understood what her heart was saying now. She was falling in love with Tyler Winter.

Tyler tightened his grip, and Lacey suddenly realized that she was afraid, afraid of losing Tyler before she learned what loving him really meant. It wasn't a game any more. She wanted his love too much. What if he didn't feel the same way? What if she were wrong about what was happening? She was scared silly.

"Think we could find a balcony around here?" he asked softly, nibbling on her ear.

"Why, do you want another lick on the head?"

"I'd chance it, just to have you jump on top of me again." Tyler whirled her around and pulled her deeper into his embrace. A smile of happiness stretched from one side of his face to the other as his agile fingers moved down her back and rubbed sensual circles at the top of her hips.

"Not fair, Tyler! Truce, remember?" Lacey tugged herself out of his arms. "I have to powder my nose," she said.

"All right," he murmured, undaunted. "I'm ready to take you someplace more private anyway. I'll pay the check and meet you at the door."

Lacey plunged though the darkness around the dance floor into the semidarkness of the lobby, pushed open the door marked Cowgirls and entered a mock corral lined with benches and split-rail fences. She splashed her face with cool water and examined the red-haired woman staring back at her from the mirror. Her hair had dried in wild curls. Her blue eyes seemed overly bright, and her cheeks were flushed as if she'd been running in the sun. She looked—she searched for the word to describe her appearance—she looked *alive*.

Part of her wanted to slip out a back exit and run, but another part of her wanted to find Tyler and pull him straight back to that dance floor. She admitted it wasn't more talk that she wanted, it was Tyler, his arms, his kisses, a lifetime of Tyler's loving. She didn't know what he had planned for later, but she was ready to stop running and let him lead the way.

He had disrupted her life and made himself a necessary part of it. In the beginning she couldn't seem to get past the wildly sensual response he elicited every time he came near her. Was she

wrong? Was what she was feeling simply an intense attraction to Tyler? No, what she was feeling toward Tyler Winter was much more. She was
willing to bet her future on it.

"I was about to send someone to check on you,"
Tyler said as she came out of the ladies' room.
He's been waiting impatiently by the door.

"Sorry," she answered stiffly.

"Are you all right?" His hand lightly capped her
elbow as they walked to the car.

Now that she'd openly acknowledged her need
for the man, she wanted him to take charge, to
show her where he wanted their relationship to
go. "Yes." She added more strongly, "Yes, I think I
am, Tyler. What do you have planned for . . .
dessert?"

Tyler missed a step on the uneven gravel in the
parking lot. "Dessert? You mean after that huge
plate of ribs, you want dessert?"

"I most certainly do." Lacey stumbled against
him, taking the opportunity as an excuse to tuck
her arm around his waist. She matched her steps
to his, feeling more confident now that they were
touching again. "I want more talk. I want . . .
dessert."

Lacey could feel the uncertainty in Tyler's manner. He couldn't know what was different about
her, only that something was. In the darkness
she smiled to herself. Up until now Tyler had
pursued her relentlessly, wooing her, then drawing back, leaving her filled with frustrations. She
wasn't some shy, frightened virgin. She was old
enough to admit her desire, and she wanted Tyler
Winter. For once she was going to put her misgiv-

ings away and let it happen. And then? She shivered as she considered the delicious possibilities.

At the car, Tyler opened the driver's door for her. She slid inside, brushing against him. She was rewarded by a peculiar look of disbelief on his face as he closed the door. Once Tyler was seated, he started the engine, and Lacey slid as close to him as the bucket seats would allow.

"I always wondered why single men preferred these seats," she said seriously. "They're such a barrier to romance."

"You're right. I can't imagine why I ever bought it. Uh, Lacey, you didn't happen to swill some Kickapoo Joy Juice when I wasn't looking, did you?"

"Nope, but it sounds interesting. Where can we get some?"

"Dogpatch." He laughed. "It's a recipe from the *Li'l Abner* comic strip. It's made from some kind of fruit juice and moonshine mixed in a washtub. You stir it with your feet."

"Feet? Yuck! I'd rather have something sweet. How about some more of that creative ice cream for dessert? You know, squirt ourselves with whipped cream and stuff."

Tyler studied her out of the corner of his eye, his expression signifying that he was not entirely certain what to make of her odd change in behavior. "Maybe you do need something cold. You feel a little warm to me."

"Just a matter of residual Tabasco sauce," she retorted flippantly, leaning across him to flick closed the lock on his door. "And a little repressed desire. Have to repress it, don't I? That's what you do when you call a truce, isn't it? Wouldn't want to arouse you, Ty."

"You call this a truce, Lacey?" Tyler shifted uncomfortably, feeling her breasts snuggled against his arm.

"Why, sure, partner, a truce means each person can speak his mind without having to worry about the other one taking advantage. No confrontation, just negotiations. I don't know why we didn't declare one earlier."

Lacey was conscious, as they pulled out of the parking lot, of Tyler's effort to devote an extra measure of attention to his driving. He was tense, handling the steering wheel as if the car were filled with nitroglycerin and they had ten miles of rough road to cover.

"Maybe the truce was a dumb idea." With newfound determination, suddenly he gave the engine a jolt of gas.

"Where're we off to in such a hurry?"

"You want dessert, crazy lady, and you're going to get it." Several minutes later he pulled into the parking lot of a swank ice cream parlor. "What flavor?"

"I feel adventurous, Ty. Surprise me."

In a few minutes he came out of the store with a large white-and-pink paper bag. He put it behind the seat, and they roared off into the traffic again.

"If we were in the van we could put it in my ice chest so it wouldn't melt before we got back to Harmony Hall," she observed.

"We aren't going that far," he said in a tight voice. Tyler swung the car onto a wide boulevard, which Lacey knew led to the governor's mansion

and some of Atlanta's most exclusive neighbor-
hoods.

"Dessert with the governor?"

Tyler turned onto a small side road canopied by
large oak trees. She noticed that his mouth had
formed a stiff line. She was confusing him. She
was confused herself. Ever since they'd left the
restaurant, she'd had an uncontrollable urge to
test him, to see if she could make him admit that
he was as uncertain as she about what was happening between them. If what they were experiencing was only sexual desire, she wanted to
know—right away.

He pulled into the parking area of a tall, luxury
apartment building, the tires squealing as he drove
through the lanes. "I think," he said grimly, "that
you know where we're going to have dessert."

He jerked the car into a space. They were totally
alone on the upper level of a brightly lit parking
facility. The sound of the engine echoed across
the emptiness.

"Just where are we, Tyler?"

"You want dessert, I'm going to give you what
you want, Lacey. For tonight, and for as long as
you'll let me."

The gentle humor in his voice was gone. He no
longer was all sweetness and light. His voice was
brusque and commanding, and when he got out
of the car and started toward the elevator, Lacey
had to double her steps to keep up with him.

They stood silently, side by side. He punched a
button and moved stiffly away from her. She
crossed her arms over her chest and wondered
anxiously if she'd unloosed a lion. Tyler carried
the bag of ice cream as if it were a shield and she

were threatening him with a sword. She didn't know how to act now that he wasn't constantly touching and kissing her. Suddenly she wished that she hadn't been quite so cavalier in her response to his efforts to be friendly.

"On second thought, Tyler, I don't believe I want dessert tonight. I made a mistake. I'd better go home and get to bed. Mother is expecting me to interview a glassblower and a leatherworker tomorrow, who want to join her merry menagerie."

"Oh, no, Lacey, this time you're not going to run away."

The elevator discharged them on the fourteenth floor. They walked a few yards down an elegant but austere hallway. Tyler stopped at a heavy paneled door and inserted his key in the lock.

The door opened. He motioned for her to step inside. As she did, she noticed that her heart was pounding erratically against her rib cage. Tyler flicked on the lights and she surveyed the apartment with a frown. Her first impression frightened her. A fireplace, overstuffed chairs, sinfully thick carpet, track lighting producing a seductive glow, a wet bar—all made the clear statement that it was a man's apartment, a man who knew how to impress a woman. Tyler closed the door behind them.

"Welcome to my home, Lacey."

An odd and painful feeling wound its way around her stomach. It was so quiet, so empty. "Is this where you bring all your ladies?" she asked.

"Where I what?"

Her hands were quivering. She clasped them together tightly. "I said, is this where you bring all the women you make love to?"

Tyler stared at her for a moment. "I've made love to a few women here, yes."

Lacey looked around at the low-slung burgundy couch, the chrome lamps, and the glass accent tables. Very cosmopolitan, very successful, very cold.

She walked across the room to the bank of windows that overlooked the city. Outside the window was a tiny balcony that reminded Lacey of standing on the Carmichael's balcony and being kissed for the first time by the man who now stood silently behind her.

"Where, Tyler?"

"Where, what?" His voice was husky, as if he were remembering too.

"Where do you make love to the ladies?"

"Damn it, Lacey, what's wrong with you?" Tyler walked into the kitchen and turned on the lights. She heard him roughly shove the ice cream into the freezer. She closed her eyes, took a deep breath, then gazed around the sumptuous living room. A dark hallway led back into the rest of the apartment. She walked quickly down the corridor, searching for a light switch. The overheard fixture illuminated a selection of doorways. Within ten seconds she'd found the master bedroom. This time she left the lights off and began removing her clothes.

"Lacey, where are you?"

"In your bedroom, Tyler."

She heard his quick, forceful steps coming down the hallway. Shivering, Lacey kept her back to the door. She was bare above the waist now. He stopped abruptly at the door.

"What the hell?" he said in a raspy voice. Tyler

switched on the recessed lighting. Light fell on his king-sized bed covered in gray satin. "Lacey, what do you think you're doing?"

"I don't know. I feel peculiar. I wanted to know how it felt to be one of your women."

"Oh, Lacey. I don't want you to be one of my women. I want you to be my only woman. But, are you sure?"

"No, I'm not sure at all. I'm scared silly. It's never mattered before."

"I know."

"What is it like, Tyler?" Lacey moved silently across the carpeted floor until she was beside him. She felt her breath grow short at the way his gaze moved over her. She reached out and flicked off the lights. Then she pushed the door closed, throwing the room into total darkness.

"Oh, Lord," Tyler whispered as Lacey placed her palms on his chest. She unbuttoned his shirt, then shoved it and his jacket off his shoulders. The clothes rustled to the floor behind him. "Are you sure you know what you're asking?"

"I'm asking you to let me kiss you, Tyler." And she did, discovering in doing so that she'd developed a definite talent for the task. His mouth opened in amazement, then remained open to accept the sensuous exploration of her tongue. By the time she pulled back, his pants were unbuttoned and the zipper was unzipped.

"Why, Tyler, no underwear?"

"Lacey," Tyler pleaded, twisting away from her embrace. "You're going to push me too far."

"But that's how all this started, isn't it? I pushed you over the banister." She moved back against him, reveling in the feel of his soft chest hair against her bare breasts.

"Ahhh! I thought that we were going to talk, get to know each other."

"Exactly. Aren't we getting to know each other, Tyler?" Lacey reached out, sliding her arms around his bare back, leaning her body against him as she allowed her fingers to play lightly up and down his spine. "Tyler?"

"What about the truce?"

"I just threw down my white flag."

"All right, my crazy lady, if making love is what you want," he replied in a ragged voice. He removed his pants, then kicked his loafers off. Then he took Lacey in a fiery embrace and claimed her mouth.

A roar of sensations swept through Lacey. A tiny gasp of pleasure escaped from her lips as Tyler found her breasts and nuzzled them.

"So lovely," he murmured. "I want so much to give you pleasure." His smooth fingertips were like pads of heat on her bare skin, and she could feel him trembling as she swept her hands across the chest she'd wanted to touch for so long. The room was absolutely silent, so the sounds of each of their whispers and movements were magnified in sensual stereo. He slid her skirt and panties down, then slowly trailed his hand across her naked stomach. Lacey whimpered as his fingers slipped between her thighs.

"So ready," he said softly as his fingers found the moist center of her desire.

"Oh, Tyler. Tyler, love me, please."

With a sudden motion, Tyler lifted her into his arms and strode toward the bed. She wrapped her arms around him, holding herself to him. Not bothering to turn back the bed covers, he placed her on her back, then lowered his body in a graceful action on top of hers. The hard, heated part of him pulsed against her abdomen, and she arched upwards. His hips moved gently, showing her how the rhythm would feel when he was inside her.

His delicious movements suddenly stopped. "Lacey, I'm afraid you'll regret this."

"Tyler, don't you dare stop. I'll regret it if you do." She clasped him tighter, arching herself once again to meet him. With a moan, he adjusted his body so that his exquisite fullness probed the tender, welcoming entrance between her thighs. Slowly, each second overflowing with sensation, he slid inside her. "Ty, oh, Ty," she whispered as the sweet pressure filled her body.

"Just a minute, darling, I ought to . . ." He raised up, and her body practically clamored its frustration.

"No, don't stop." She tightened her grip and arched against him.

"Lacey, you're going to make me . . ."

"Oh, Tyler. I want . . . I want . . ."

She kissed him and let her body begin the ancient rhythm. Lacey let herself rise in a pulsating spiral of desire. Higher and higher they climbed, until the explosion that followed sent a thousand strands of pleasure through her. It was the most beautiful experience she'd ever known in her life.

"Ty, it was wonderful." Lacey dimly heard her own words and knew how woefully inadequate they were. He was kissing her neck, and his hands reached between their bodies to stroke her gently.

"Dammit, Lacey," he whispered. "That was crazy."

"Wasn't it, though? Crazy, wonderful. Oh, Tyler. I had no idea. Don't you dare move."

"Lacey darling, there's nothing I'd like better than to stay right here, inside you, but I'm afraid that we've just done something very foolish. Now we definitely need to talk."

Lacey crossed her legs around him. He drew his head back and looked down at her in the darkness. She clasped his face between her hands and pulled him close so that she could nibble his mouth. "For once, Tyler, what I want is to kiss, not talk."

"Lacey, Lacey . . ."

"Ssssh."

She moved under her and felt him growing firm inside her again. By the time she stopped kissing him, he'd begun to answer her movements once more.

"Lacey, I never want to hurt you." Tyler tensed his muscles, and she could tell he was trying desperately to control the rhythmic flexing in his lower body. His breath was coming a little gasps. "This isn't smart, darling."

"I think it's the smartest thing I've ever done. Touch me, Tyler. Touch my breasts. I want to feel every inch of you touching every inch of me."

"Lord, I've created a lovely monster." He braced himself on his elbows and dipped his head so that he could take one of her nipples in his mouth, teasing, and caressing until she thought she would disintegrate from the heat of her desire.

She groaned. "I can't get enough of you, Tyler. Hurry." She arched against him. He plunged uncontrollably into her writhing body, murmuring words of love. It took her a few minutes to realize that each thrust was accompanied by a whispered "love you, love you, love you." As the pace increased he said her name, over and over, drawn out with soft moans. Lacey whispered ecstatic encouragement.

This time when he collapsed against her, Lacey relaxed, sated, drained, filled with a satisfaction that permeated every cell in her body. But when Tyler started to move away, again she tried to hold him.

"No, darling. Let me go. I'll be right back," he urged.

Lacey closed her eyes and let her hands trail over his shoulders as he left her. She heard the sound of his footsteps, the opening of a door, and the running of water. When he came back he was carrying a towel and a warm, wet washcloth. He sat down beside her and gently slid the cloth between her legs.

"Tyler, don't. I like the idea that part of you is still in me."

His hand paused. She heard him sigh wearily. "I know what I'm doing now is probably a worthless effort. You realize, Lacey, that you stopped me from taking any precautions. Part of me may very well be in you. What if I've made you pregnant?"

She lay there for a long silent moment. Pregnant? The possibility had crossed her mind, but at the time nothing had mattered except what was happening between them. Dumb? Perhaps. Tyler wasn't her first lover, but he'd been the first in a very long time. As much as she'd been taught and had read about sexual responsibility, she'd allowed herself to be carried away. Perhaps the risk she'd taken had been a subconscious wish for a way to bind him to her. She shifted her body, feeling the warm, intimate moisture as he stroked the washcloth over her.

"It's all right, darling," he whispered. "I like taking care of you."

A baby, Lacey thought numbly. How strange that she'd never in her life though of herself making a baby. Dolls, yes, but babies? How wonderful, she thought. And then she knew that she could love a baby, Tyler's baby. She refused to think about it further. For now their physical relationship was enough.

"Don't worry, Tyler," she said softly. "I'm not going to be pregnant."

Tyler sat there in the darkness, his hand resting on her thigh. She could feel his indecision.

"I don't know what to say, Lacey. You know that I've wanted you from the first moment I kissed you at the wedding. It started off as fun, a nice way to enjoy an afternoon, but it's more than that now. I think you feel the same way."

"Yes," she said simply.

"I guess I haven't had much time for a real relationship with a woman, until now. I won't apologize for what just happened. I will apologize for not taking it slower and easier for you. Next time it will be better, I promise."

Relationships? Slower? Lacey wasn't sure how to answer him. She trembled, and quipped with a giggle. "Next time? When do you think that'll be?"

"Not long. I don't think it will be long at all," Tyler promised, lying back down beside her and taking her in his arms. "But for now, we'll just snuggle, all right?"

"All right," she whispered.

It wasn't until she was back in her bed at Harmony Hall that she remembered the words he'd spoken as passion overwhelmed them, ". . . love you, love you, love you . . ." Lacey frowned. She refused to dissect her feeling for Tyler. Whether it was love or desire, it was wonderful. Mother had said a Wilcox woman would know when she'd met the right man. Hormones didn't account for the deep sense of belonging she'd felt in Tyler's arms.

No matter what happened, she knew that her life had become complicated in ways she hadn't ever dreamed of, and a deep sense of wonder began to grow inside her.

Seven

Making love to Tyler hadn't solved anything. It had only proved to her that his touch was addictive. Her compulsion to see him was intense, beginning the moment she opened her eyes to the bright sunshine spilling across her bed. When he'd brought her home the night before, she'd maintained a sophisticated, nonchalant attitude. She'd kissed him good night at the door, trying not to let her anguish show. She'd done fine, until he'd caught her arm and stopped her as she was turning to go inside.

"Lacey," he'd asked hesitantly. "do . . . do you like children?"

"Of course. I think that's why I love my dolls so much. Why?"

"So do I," he said firmly. "There was a time, once, when I thought that having a child would be wonderful but . . ." His voice trailed off. He'd looked at her for a long minute. "I knew something special was happening between us." A bittersweet smile came to his face. He kissed her once more and left.

She should have been happy. It should have given her hope that he was serious about a commitment. She thought of Callie and the child she would bear Matt. Could Tyler know about Callie's child? No, Callie had said that she and Matt had kept their joy to themselves.

But Tyler's words didn't reassure her, they only made her panic. Children? Could two people meet and learn to care for each other in so short a time? Lacey was afraid to call it love. She wasn't sure she knew what love was—not yet.

Lacey threw her feet over the edge of her bed and forced herself to sit up. Her body gave her gentle reminders of what she and Tyler had shared the night before. She sighed. The pain she was feeling was mental, not physical. She wasn't used to dealing with emotional decisions. All her life she'd had to be the practical one, making decisions based on clear-cut needs and demands. For once in her life could she allow her heart to run free?

Lacey showered and wandered down to the kitchen, dabbing at her forehead in the sticky summer heat. Pinned to the refrigerator was a note from her parents explaining that they wouldn't be home till early afternoon. From the barn at the back of the house she heard the chipping sound of a mallet. Mr. Spragg, she thought. Giving a ladylike tug to the legs of her cut off jeans and the hem of her faded T-shirt, Lacey slid her feet into a pair of old flip-flops she kept by the screened porch, and ran out into the bright morning sunlight.

"Mr. Spragg?"

The round little man lowered his mallet and slid his glasses to the top of his bare, pink head.

"Morning, Lacey. What do you think of my duck?"

Lacey studied the chunk of wood with its gouged-out sections. "This is what we were looking for the other day? This thing is a duck?" The words slipped out before she could mask her astonishment.

"Well, not really. But it's the essence of all nature, it's nature's spirit—or it will be when I'm done—a tribute to the vanishing woodlands, to nature in all her glory. Spence is the one who nicknamed it my duck."

"Oh, yes, I see. Well, hmmm, Mr. Spragg, do you know where everybody is?"

"After he participated in morning meditation, I believe your young man and your mother went into town."

"Tyler? He was here? He meditated with you?"

Mr. Spragg nodded. "He came by very early. He appears to be a very sensitive young man. He said he used to meditate regularly."

Lacey stared at him in amazement. "Why did Tyler and my mother go into town?"

"To meet the glassblower."

"I wish someone had called me before they left. Is something wrong with Mother's car? I just don't understand why Tyler went with her."

"Tyler was insistent on letting you sleep in."

"And my father?"

"Alfred left a few minutes ago with the gentleman who is selling him the polo pony."

"Polo pony! I'll see you later, Mr. Spragg." Lacey broke into a run toward the van.

"I'm afraid you're too late to catch them, Lacey. And I don't know where the pony is being stabled," he called out. Her run slowed to a dejected walk. "But don't worry, your father is going to pay for the pony out of his advance from his book on General Lee."

Lacey held her head with her hands. Her father had been compiling research on his book for twenty-five years. So far as Lacey knew, he had yet to write a single word.

Considering the sleepless night she'd spent, she knew she was up against an impossible situation. She was practically walking in a fog, while Tyler bustled about involving himself in everything at Harmony Hall. He was becoming a member of her family, and she wasn't sure how she felt about it. She wasn't sure how she felt about Tyler. Would he expect a repeat performance of last night? Of course he would, and if she were here when he returned, she wouldn't be able to stop herself from making love with him again. Even now she wanted . . .

She wouldn't dwell on it; she'd simply pack up and leave for a few days. Her family wouldn't be surprised. She was on the road more than she was at home anyway. She had her little warehouse and studio in the back of a friend's fabric shop up in the mountains to go to. She'd pick up the dolls for the Junebug Festival in Cherokee County and deliver new supplies to her seamstresses. Tyler would get over his fascination with her family and be gone by the time she got back.

Lacey was writing a note when Arthur came into the kitchen rubbing his whiskered chin and yawning.

"Morning Lace. Where is everybody?"

"Everybody had gone somewhere. Tell Mother that I have to go pick up supplies. I'll see her in a few days, maybe."

"Fine." Arthur munched cereal as he watched Lacey. "And what do I tell Tyler?"

"Tell him . . . tell him if he gets tired of my family, I'll understand. I'm going to find myself a balcony to jump off of."

"What?"

"Never mind, Arthur. Just tell them I'll be back in a few days."

"Are you running away, sis?"

"Of course not. I'm just taking a little time to . . . to get in touch with my true feelings."

Tyler might think he could adjust to the Wilcoxes, but Lacey knew better, and it would be easier on her family if she put a stop to Tyler's intrusion now, before they began to depend on him. Who was she kidding? She was running away. It wasn't her family she was concerned about. For once it was Lacey she was protecting, Lacey who had to find a way to understand and come to terms with her feelings for Tyler, before she ended up wounded in the skirmish.

Six days and five restless nights later, Lacey gave in and drove home. Nothing seemed the same. Her dolls, her friends, her easy relationship with her seamstresses—everything seemed off-key. All she could think about was Tyler and how much she wanted to be with him. Finally she'd given up and faced the truth. She hadn't left Tyler behind. He'd been with her every second of every day. The drive home had never seemed so long. She didn't know where their relationship was headed, but she knew she wanted what Callie and Matt had, and she wanted it with Tyler.

She parked the lavender van in its regular spot beneath the oak tree, and glanced around in amazement. The grass had been neatly mowed. New lattice-work walls adorned the gazebo, and the copper rooster was now standing upright on its lightning rod atop the *freshly painted?* barn.

From the barn came the sounds of vigorous hammering and sawing. Dear heavens, had Mr. Spragg's duck become a full flock? Or had her mother taken off on a rebuilding tangent? she wondered. No, her father must be renovating the barn for the polo pony. He'd decided to buy the pony after all. Lacey began to run.

Inside the barn she came to an abrupt stop. The center section had a new floor. The stalls now had walls from the floor to a new, lower ceiling. The center aisle was open to a new roof that had been inset with panels of clear glass, flooding the building with natural light. There was no sign of a pony. Inside the first cubicle, Lacey found Mr. Spragg arranging tools on a pegboard wall over a brightly painted workbench.

"Mr. Spragg, what's happening here?"

"Isn't it wonderful? We're each going to have our own studio."

"Who?"

"Why, Phillip, and me, Dawn the glassblower, and your brother, Arthur. Ty has even planned a space for your workshop, and a studio for himself as well."

"Ty?"

Lacey felt a sick foreboding begin in the pit of her stomach. Tyler was still here. That was good. But he hadn't been waiting there for her. He'd done what she'd been most afraid of—fallen deeper into the Wilcox craziness. "What does Tyler have to do with this?"

"He's organizing and planning our new co-operative."

Spence walked—not tapped—his way into the barn. "And I'm going to be the business manager and handle bookings and sales," he said proudly. He carried what looked like a computer. "We're going to produce, expand, become self-sufficient. Lacey, isn't it wonderful?"

"Yes, indeed," Mr. Spragg agreed cheerfully. "Instead of ducks, I'm going to make hand-carved signs and plaques. We'll sell them at craft shows and flea markets, like your dolls. Ty seems to think my work will sell well."

"But what about your duck, your tribute to the vanishing wildlife?" Lacey stared helplessly as Spence carried his computer into what appeared to be a small office on the opposite side of the corridor.

"Oh, I'll still work on my art in my spare time," Mr. Spragg said. "But for now, we have to get the barn ready to open to the public on weekends, after we've added a couple of more tenants."

"What do you think?" Spence interjected.

"I think I'd like to talk to Mr. Winter," Lacey said, trying to hold back the resentment she felt boiling up inside her. It was supposed to be *her* Tyler wanted, not her family. How dare he step in and take over. It was her responsibility, not his—not yet. He should never have taken such a step without consulting her. "Where is he?"

"Down in your studio putting up shelves," Mr. Spragg said. "I'm making name plates for each studio, Lacey." She strode toward the back of the barn. "What will you call your shop?"

She didn't answer because she couldn't trust herself to speak. Following the sound of an electric saw in a building which had, up to now, never been wired for electricity, Lacey marched the length of the barn into a large, bright, open room which smelled of fresh paint and sawdust. Beowulf lay sprawled in a patch of sunlight beneath a sparkling new window. Miranda slept curled between the big Dane's front legs.

Tyler, clad in faded cutoffs, red socks, and tea-colored leather work boots, was standing with his bare, sweaty back to her, working. He'd tied a red bandana around his head, threading it through his dark mass of hair as if he were a renegade Indian. Light-colored wood shavings frosted his hair like shards of sunlight and they peppered his strong arms.

The man she was watching lift a board into place above a counter was no yuppie. The man she was watching was no smooth talking real estate executive. The man she was watching was magnificently male, and her heart and her hormones sent off rockets as she fought to keep from flinging herself into his arms. She was confused and angry, and she didn't stop to analyze her furious reaction.

"Mr. Winter! What do you think you're doing?"

Tyler turned around, let out a whoop of joy, and covered the distance between them in three steps. "Lacey love! You're back." Before she could utter another word, he swung her into the air, whirled her around, and smothered her words of protest with his lips.

She wasn't going to return his kiss until he explained what he was doing. She wasn't going to acknowledge the jolt of sheer pleasure that swept through her traitorous body. She'd show him a thing or two about high-handedness. It was time he learned he wasn't in charge.

She spent at least thirty seconds firmly ignoring the man, the next ten seconds admitting that she was woefully inadequate at indifference, and the next ten seconds acknowledging that what she was doing was what she'd done every time he kissed her—kissing him back. By the time she'd finished showing him her true feelings, both his hands were definitely very high on her body, and her breasts were registering every touch of his fingertips.

"This is your studio, Lacey. Do you like it? I've painted it the color of sunshine, because that's how I think of you, darling. What do you think?" he asked.

"You what?" Her lips felt swollen, and she found it hard to talk. Sometime during her attempt at keeping her distance, her arms had disobeyed and crept around his neck. He lifted her lovingly and sat her on the work table.

"My studio is directly over yours. Of course it will take me a while to have anything ready to sell, so my studio won't be open to the public for a while."

"You're going to have a realtor's office in the top of our barn?"

He laughed. "Not real estate. I'm going to be a real estate consultant now. The rest of the time I'm going to be an artist in residence, at least part-time. I've missed you, Lacey. It's been pure hell. I'm so glad you're back. I've been sleeping in your bed." He frowned at her. "I'm trying not to worry or be possessive, but if you stay away again, I'll come after you."

His lean fingers tightened on her shoulders and slowly and deliberately drew her back into his embrace. "Stop being afraid of me, Lacey, and show me how glad you are to see me."

She closed her eyes, breathing in the hot, warm smell of the sawdust, the sunlight, and the man. "Don't, Tyler. Please don't. I'm not an experienced woman of the world. I don't know how to stop myself from showing you. I just know everything is happening too fast. I'm . . . afraid."

Tyler shivered, tightened his arms for a moment, and then sighed as he pulled away. "Stop fighting me, Lacey. There's no use in trying to pretend that you don't care for me. I know better. There is nothing wrong. Your fears, not your heart, are causing you to talk this way."

Lacey lowered her head. If she couldn't see the naked need in his eyes, she might be able to draw her wits about her. Looking down was a mistake. Her line of vision went straight down Tyler's aroused body to the part of him that she wanted most to avoid.

"You're right, Tyler. I've made up my mind not to pretend anymore. That's why I feel so vulnerable. What are you doing here? I—we don't need you to take care of us. What do you want from us, from me?"

"I really am going to live here, right here in my studio, until I can convince you to live here with me. Lacey, don't you understand? I'm in love with you."

"But why, Tyler? What could you possible find in me to entice you to give up your job and return to the bohemian painter's life you gave up in disgust? I think you've flipped out. It isn't me you want. You're having some kind of mid-life crisis. You don't belong here."

"A mid-life crisis at thirty? No, Lacey. I do belong here, darling. You're funny. You're warm. You're loyal and caring and incredibly sexy. From the moment you took a nose dive over that banister and jumped on me at the wedding, I thought you were special. And then when I came here and met your family, and saw how hard you were working all by yourself, I knew you were the person I'd been looking for all my life."

"But, Tyler, you don't have to court me to be with my family. As you can see, they take in any needy stray. You don't have to pretend to be an artist again. You don't have to love me to—Oh, I'm saying this so badly!"

She finally understood what Tyler was saying. He thought he couldn't impress her family without talent. Without talent he couldn't stay at Harmony Hall, and he wanted to be a part of the Wilcoxes' lives, to share their life-style. Perhaps he was getting older and felt the need to relive his carefree college days. In order to do all those things, he had to exhibit both a talent and an interest in their daughter.

"You may not believe this, my crazy gypsy lady, but I care about you, and I really do want to be an artist again. I was serious when I told you there was a time, long ago, when I wanted to become the next Picasso. You've made me realize I haven't given up that goal. I don't have to be a business-man here. I can be me, and you can be my inspi-ration. Inspire me, Lacey Lee Wilcox."

"But, Tyler . . ."

He covered her mouth with his, slowly, insis-tently. He nudged her into acceptance as his tongue probed her lips apart. She couldn't refuse him. From the very first time he'd kissed her, she'd given as much as she'd received. Her tongue tan-gled with his, and she knew she was right where she wanted to be.

"Ah, sweet," he murmured, his fingers stroking her back. "I want to do this forever."

"I thought I'd come back today to find you'd lost interest in me." She closed her eyes, knowing she'd die if he didn't care for her too.

"Lose interest in you? Ah, darling Lacey," he said gently. "I've had one eye on this barn and the other on the road ever since you left. I mean it when I say I'd follow you if you ever took off again. I wanted to go after you this time."

"Why didn't you?"

"Your mother convinced me that you needed time

to think. She said you always weighed all the facts before you decided what to do. Did you come back to me, Lacey?"

She looked up at him in stunned delight. Could he really mean what he was saying about caring, about staying here and becoming a permanent part of her life? Lacey suddenly realized she could live with the fear that her marvelous dream might fade. She'd enjoy the dream and pray for it to last.

"Yes . . . yes, yes, yes. Oh, Tyler," she whispered, letting her feelings find a voice. "I really do love you."

"Ah, Lacey Lee. Lovely Lacey Lee . . . I love you, too, love you so much . . ." He kissed her as he'd never kissed her before, deeply, passionately, reverently, saying much more with his kiss than he ever could with words. She leaned further back on the counter top, drawing him closer.

"Hey, Ty, I need more nails."

Tyler quickly pulled his mouth from hers. He took an awkward step back and looked at Spence, who stood in the doorway. Lacey shot upright and climbed off the table. Spence smiled at the two of them sheepishly. Tyler coughed. "In the truck, Spence." Lacey heard the desire in this voice. She looked at the ceiling to avoid Spence's gaze, and she felt a blush warming her face.

"Well . . . er . . . well . . . happy . . . work . . . bye," Spence stammered, and left.

Lacey smoothed her T-shirt and fanned herself. Thank goodness for Spence's intrusion. She might have let Tyler make love to her out in the open, within shouting distance of other people. Something about Tyler's last remark had struck her as odd, and she gradually sifted the words through her mind. He took her back in his arms and began nibbling her lower lip.

"Truck? What truck? Tyler Winter, I insist that you stop kissing me and tell me what's going on here."

"You're right, darling. I've got so much to show you. We're getting organized here. Everyone's going to sell his or her work and become self-supporting."

"But, Tyler, who gave you permission to turn our barn into some kind of commune? And where'd we get a truck?"

"I traded my sports car for a pickup. It seemed more practical."

Her voice was filled with resigned amusement and a hint of sarcasm. "I suppose you're Andy of Mayberry, and the truck came with a gun rack and a fishing pole, and little Opie will pop up any minute? Are you going to change everything around here?"

Tyler stood dead still. "Lacey, I'm sorry. I should have waited to discuss it with you, but I wanted it to be a surprise. I was just helping out your family, trying to make life easier for you."

"Tyler, my family and I aren't a package deal. You don't have to do this. I can take care of my folks, and I can take care of me. I always have."

"I know," he admitted in a low voice.

"I don't need you to be responsible for my family." Her stern voice had faded to a sob. She knew she was overreacting, but she couldn't stop herself. He looked so hurt. "Oh, I'm sorry Tyler. I sound terribly ungrateful and I'm not. You're confusing me. I'm sorry, Tyler."

He stepped away and simply stared at her for a long anguished minute before answering, "I just wanted to help you. I'm sorry." He brushed his hair away from his face. "I wanted you, and I believed if I proved to you that I could fit into your life, you'd feel the same about me. But it's not the same thing, is it? I mean you want me, but not as a part of your life here at Harmony Hall."

"Lacey! Lacey, are you out here?" Gynneth swept into the barn. She wore her excitement like a new gown. "Isn't this wonderful? Tyler has managed to create what I've envisioned all along. My dream is finally going to be realized, thanks to this dear, dear man."

Lacey looked at the man responsible for her mother's happiness. "Tyler is an efficient organizer," she said stiffly. "He knows how to handle people."

"We'll have people at Harmony Hall again. Arthur is going to have a music studio and give lessons when he isn't composing. And maybe, maybe Medina will come home. Oh, it's a miracle, and it's all because of your wonderful young man."

Medina? Come home? She'd never even considered the possibility.

Gynneth was right. Tyler had managed to accomplish what she hadn't. He'd motivated the residents and her brother into taking the steps necessary to become self-sufficient.

"It's all Tyler's idea," Gynneth raved, "and with each resident having his own studio out here, even your father has gotten caught up in the effort. He's taken on the cooking—and can you believe that he's actually started his biography of General Lee?"

"He has?"

"Indeed," Gynneth said. "Of course, he'll have to have a secretary do the actual typing, but he's begun. Lacey, she won't be terribly expensive to employ and she'll act as my social secretary as well."

"Of course, you would need a secretary," Lacey agreed with a tight smile.

"And, Lacey, we do understand about Tyler. I mean, your father and I will try to be open-minded about your relationship if you— I mean, well, he is certainly a fine young man. We thought so even before we knew what a motivator he is. Did you know that it was Tyler who took care of that snippy young woman at the phone company?"

"Now, Gynneth, perhaps we ought not to over-whelm Lacey," Tyler said anxiously. "All these changes have come as a shock to her."

"Shock? Of course not," Lacey answered in a voice so choked that she could hardly speak. "I'm very pleased that you two seem to work so well together. Would either of you like to explain how we are going to pay for all this? Or has Tyler covered that too?" Lacey knew she was being un-reasonable. The expression on her mother's face reflected how petulant and ungrateful her words sounded.

"Why, Lacey, I'm surprised at you. You sound positively rude. Don't pay any attention to her, Tyler. She always acts this way when I do things without discussing them with her first. Though I really don't know why. I am her mother, and I'm perfectly capable of making wise decisions on my own."

"Of course you are, Mother." Lacey said slowly. "It isn't that I'm not impressed with your plans. I'm just—I'm just surprised, I guess. Forget what I said, Tyler. I was overreacting. You have done a magnificent job here."

Aware that he had every reason to turn and walk out of the barn and away from Harmony Hall, Lacey held her breath until she saw his lips began to curve stiffly.

"No, Lacey, you are absolutely right. What you see is only phase one of my plan. You and I need to talk about the rest, in private.'"

"Tyler, the rock man is here with the gravel for the parking area!" Arthur called from the yard.

"In private?" Lacey questioned with a sardonic smile.

"Right." Tyler looked around, then turned back to her. "Will you let me get cleaned up and take you to dinner? We can talk without interruption then." He smiled and his whole face turned into a plea, a plea Lacey couldn't ignore.

"To dinner?" He was doing it again, confusing her with his change of direction. He was like a bumper car in the amusement park, charging into a crowd, running into a log jam, and charging off to come at his victim from another direction.

"Yes, there's still a freezer full of ice cream that we haven't tasted yet. I seem to remember we never quite got around to it before. You don't mind, do you, Gynneth?" he asked. "It's Alfred's turn to cook anyway."

Lacey blinked slowly. "I don't believe it. My father is actually cooking?"

"Not only that, but he repaired the gazebo,"

Gynneth said proudly. "At least, he hired a young college student from the polo stable to come out and repaint it while he supervised."

"All right, Tyler. Anybody who can convince my father to cook deserves to be listened to. I have to unpack the van. Shall we say dinner in about one hour?"

"Sure." He grinned. "Just shove my things off your bed. You can shower first."

"Your things, on my bed? You've really been sleeping in my bed?"

"Only for a couple of nights. It saved me the trouble of having to drive back and forth." He raised his head, deliberately focusing the full force of his dark eyes upon her. She wished he hadn't. She wished he'd get a haircut—a crewcut—so that she wouldn't feel the urge to run her fingers through the swatch of hair that seemed forever draped across his forehead.

"You do want the shower first, don't you?" His voice was saying shower, but his eyes were recalling memories of her in his bed, and both of them knew exactly what he was thinking.

"Yes. I'll try to hurry and get out of your way."

"Well, you two work it out," Gynneth said lightly. "I'm sure you'll figure out a way to share the facilities. I'll just slip into the kitchen and check on Alfred. He's preparing pheasant under glass. Can you imagine, I had to drive all the way into Atlanta to find fresh pheasant? Everybody is going to love his special recipe."

Gynneth glided out of the barn, humming.

"Pheasant?" Lacey shook her head in disbelief.

"Well, they're your parents," Tyler said helplessly.

"There's just so much reprogramming I can do. I'm not infallible."

"Good, I was beginning to wonder if you could be stopped."

"I can't be stopped, but I can be slowed, darling Lacey. After dinner we can decide just how far you want me to go, and how fast."

"Maybe I was wrong about my reaction to what you've accomplished. I'll listen to your plans. I may have some of my own."

Maybe the expression on his face before she walked out of the barn was one of skepticism. Maybe his expression was one of restrained anticipation. The water in her shower wasn't cold enough, she decided, as she considered her maybes. Maybe she'd let loose a handsome dragon.

Eight

There was a light tap on her door. "Lacey?"

"Tyler?" Without a thought she opened her door and drew him inside, hurling herself into his arms. "I'm not ready to go yet."

"Lord," he said with a sigh. "Forget going. Forget food. If you'll keep holding me like this, we'll never go to dinner." He looked down at the expression on her face. "Lord," he whispered again, wondering if she knew that everything she was thinking was reflected in her gaze.

"Can't we go someplace, right now?" she asked breathlessly.

He nodded. "I know a perfect place."

"What shall I wear?"

"Forget the clothes," he said with a wicked expression. "I don't think you'll need them, not if you'll settle for pizzas, delivered—later." She nodded. He took her hand and pulled her behind him, tiptoeing carefully down the steps past the kitchen where Alfred was taking a broiling pan out of the oven.

"These pheasant are browning nicely." Alfred was wearing a tall, white chef's hat and a white apron. "What shall I serve them on?"

"What about our crystal cake-plate, darling? The cover ought to fit over the birds nicely."

"Wonderful, Gynneth. I'll mound the rice on the plate around the birds. You melt the cheese for the asparagus."

"Do you want candles, Alfred?"

Lacey couldn't help smiling. Her parents had never seemed more content. She and Tyler slid past the open doorway and ran lightly outside, smothering their giggles like children.

"Truck or van?" Tyler asked.

"Oh, the truck, of course. I want to check out your gun rack."

"You may be disappointed. I'm working on it, but I'm not yet a good ol' boy."

"Disappointed? Never. I like good ol' executive boys."

"The kind who hang duckhead umbrellas and briefcases from their gun racks?"

"Absolutely." Lacey had left all her reservations back in her bedroom. She wasn't going to fight her feelings any longer. Suddenly she was free and eager. Wherever Tyler Winter was going was fine with her.

Tyler opened the driver's door on his truck and lifted her hand to direct her inside. As she slid past him into the cab, he reached out and gave her a quick kiss, then slid in behind her, curving one arm around her shoulders to hold her close to him.

"No bucket seats, doll. What do you think?"

"Hey, how are you going to drive?" she asked.

"I don't know. I always wondered how the kids did this." She started to move to her own side. "Don't you dare slide over there. I've got you back, and I want to keep you close."

Lacey looked at him. She could hardly breath. He was so handsome. He'd shed his three-piece suit and donned working man's garb without a thought. His hair was still frosted with sawdust, and there was a slash of yellow paint on his T-shirt. But she noticed something now that she hadn't noticed in her irate mood before—his aura of peaceful happiness. He was smiling, relaxed. She slid even closer and was rewarded with a look of pure pleasure.

"Where's your Stetson, cowboy?"

"No Stetson. Will a baseball cap do?" He pulled a battered Atlanta Braves cap from under the seat and put it on his head. He started the truck, managed to operate the straight shift with one hand, and got them started down the road in the twilight.

"How did you do it, Tyler?"

"Do what?"

"Turn my family into ordinary people? Well, maybe that's an overstatement. Let's say . . . into people who're motivated to take care of themselves?"

"Your mother and I reached an understanding. I found out what she really wanted, and she agreed to cooperate with my plan for Harmony Hall."

Lacey winced. Tyler found out what her family wanted and began to plan toward working it out. She'd never done that. She'd worked to keep up with what she'd considered her mother's foolishness, and she'd made few efforts to disguise her reservations. How she must have dampened her mother's enthusiasm.

Yet her mother and father never said anything except to tell her she mustn't feel so responsible for them. She'd wanted to care for them, she realized. They had become her self-appointed responsibility, the motivating factor in her life. What if she'd been using them all along? Did she need them to need her? Lacey stared out the truck window, caught up in confusion.

"What bargain did you make with Mother, Ty?"

"I have a publishing friend in New York who will read her poetry."

"You're kidding. Mother's poetry? Have you ever heard any of Mother's poetry?"

"Lacey, darling. You and I are absolutely perfectly matched. We share the same opinions, the same toothpaste, which I noticed on your dresser, and the same"—he slid his arm around her and massaged her breast with his strong fingers—"desire. But one thing we don't share is a bad opinion of your mother's poetry."

"But—"

"Forget about your family and Harmony Hall. Tonight just think about us. You and me, my lovely gypsy lady."

Lacey arranged her body so that Tyler could drive and easily keep his hand on her breast. At the next traffic light she changed the floorshift expertly, laughing as they roared off in a sudden spurt of power when the light changed. Thirty minutes later, Tyler drove recklessly into the parking area of his building, brought the truck to a screeching halt, and practically dragged Lacey from the cab.

"But I thought we were going to discuss Phase Two of your master plan, Ty."

"Exactly," he said as the elevator doors closed. He clamped her body to him, then lowered his mouth to claim the very breath she breathed. By the time the elevator reached the fourteenth floor, Lacey's blouse was open, Tyler's jeans were half unsnapped, and both of them failed to notice when the door opened. It began to close again. "Whoops!" Tyler exclaimed. He wedged himself between the two sides, then pulled Lacey after him as the doors obediently opened again.

Inside his apartment they kissed their way to the bedroom, removing each other's clothes along the way. Tyler placed her reverently on the bed and stood over her, his face lined with a deep frown.

"What's wrong, Tyler?"

"Wrong? Nothing, absolutely nothing. I've just wanted you here in my bed again so badly that I've dreamed you here. When you didn't come back, I moved into your bedroom so I could be close to you. And now you're here, and I feel like a nervous kid."

Lacey felt a pang of deep joy inside her began to radiate outward like the widening circle of a fire burning away from its source. "I wanted you, too, Tyler. I tried to fight it, to pretend it was just physical attraction, but it isn't. You're right. We do have something special between us. Love me, Tyler. Mother was right about a Wilcox woman knowing when she's found the man she wants."

"I want you, Lacey. But I want more than just

tonight. I want the now and forever kind of joining."

He still stood over her, his dark eyes stormy with imprisoned passion, his body showing its ripe need as he waited for her answer.

Lacey's eyes widened. "But we're already joined, Tyler, with an invisible bond that kept me tied to you even when I was gone. You were there every second of every minute as surely as if you were beside me. Please, Tyler"—she searched his eyes for a very long time—"love me."

"Yes, it has to be." His voice was gruff with passion. "I have to love you right now." He lowered himself over her, moaning as their skin touched, trembling as he parted her legs and quickly slid inside her.

"Oh, Tyler." She arched against him, the look of devotion so evident on her face that he knew without a doubt she was being truthful when she said she loved him. Their passion caught fire, ending in a desperate release.

"Darling, uninhibited wench," Tyler said, pulling back, breathing heavily as he allowed his gaze to sweep over her. "You're so very beautiful."

He tried to move away, but she held him tightly. "Don't you want me anymore, Tyler?" She gave a little wiggle of invitation. "I want you, Tyler Winter, for tonight, tomorrow, for as long as you want me too."

"That, my darling Lacey, will be forever." Tyler began to move against her once more, slowly, worshiping her body with incredible gentleness. He knew she was his. He just wasn't sure how he'd keep her once she knew the reason behind his efforts at Harmony Hall. He pushed the thought from his mind. Tonight was theirs. He captured her mouth with his and gave in to the wonderful sensations sweeping through him.

"Ty!" Lacey nearly screamed as she writhed in waves of ecstasy. Tyler could hold back no longer. He joined her willingly, clasping her to him as they soared over the edge of control and fell headlong into one long wave of pleasure. She relaxed beneath him, her eyes filled with new tears of joy over the beauty of what they'd shared.

Tyler rolled onto his back, carrying her with him. He kissed her softly, then arranged her body so that her face lay against the thick dark hair on his chest.

"You know, we'll never be able to do this at Harmony Hall," he told her with a smile.

"We won't? Oh, I guess it might not be proper." She couldn't conceal the disappointment in her voice.

"Oh, I think it's very proper, Lacey love. It's just that you're a noisy wench. You're incredibly exciting, but noisy."

She was embarrassed as she recalled her uninhibited vocal display. "Oh, I'm sorry."

"Don't be sorry, darling. I hope that I'll always be able to make you shout in joy. I love you to be noisy. I love everything about you in my bed, in my arms, in my life."

"Oh, Tyler. Are you sure? Making love with you is so wonderful. Is it always so wonderful for you?"

"No, darling." He kissed her and pulled her further over him. "It's only wonderful with us."

They lay for a time, two halves to a whole, arms and legs entangled, content to be together.

"I guess we're physically compatible, aren't we

Tyler? I mean all our parts fit together like they're meant to." Lacey raised herself up and grinned impishly at the man beneath her. Her lower body slid back a fraction of an inch. She didn't have to move any further to discover that Tyler's body was ready for her, waiting impatiently.

"Oh, compatible, yes," Tyler said coyly. "Of course, there are many other ways of being compatible. I guess we'd better check them all out before we make a firm decision on the subject." He caught Lacey's hips and lifted her a fraction.

"I don't think it will be hard to decide," she whispered as she felt glorious tingles of anticipation.

Lacey's breath caught as she felt the tip of him against her. He quivered in readiness beneath her. "I really think you'd better check and be sure," he urged hoarsely. "I wouldn't want you to consider me a poor fit."

He lowered her body slowly onto the hard, throbbing part of him. She felt a ripple of pleasure as he began to move inside her. Her hips rocked languidly, causing him to shudder from the sensation. Lacey suddenly realized how much sweet power she held over him, as her slightest motions made him moan in pleasure. His hands gripped her thighs, holding her tightly as he plunged into her.

Lacey's neck arched back as she became lost in the rhythm of their passion. She dug her fingers into his shoulders and tried to restrain the storm that threatened to break her apart.

"Don't hold back," Tyler begged. "Let go. Be as wild as you want. Don't be quiet."

But it was Tyler who cried out as his body exploded inside hers. Lacey clasped his sides as pleasure lifted her to a level of dazed ecstasy where all she recognized were his hoarse words, the same words she'd heard before.

". . . love you, love you, love you . . ."

A long time later, half dozing, she became aware that they were still joined together—damp, satiated, complete. She nudged Tyler's cheek with her lips. "Hmmm?" he responded in a blissful, sleepy tone.

"About dinner," she whispered into his ear. "Are you planning to starve me? Is that the way a man tames the woman he . . . I mean . . ." She'd almost said *loves*, but she bit back the words. She was suddenly shy about saying the words herself.

"The woman he loves." Tyler put a period to the sentence with a sigh of contentment. She settled beside him and they cuddled for a minute. Then he slid his feet over the side of the bed, drawing her up along with him as he stood. "The woman he tames," he teased. "I might keep you barefoot and pregnant, darling. Does that sound terribly chauvinistic? Would you object if I wanted you barefoot and pregnant?"

He lifted her legs around his hips and walked toward the bathroom, carrying her.

"I can walk," she protested mildly.

"I know, but I don't want to let you go. You didn't answer my question." He turned on the shower and waited as the water heated. His hands held her bare bottom and he began rubbing her up and down against him. He bent his head down to suck first one of her nipples, then the other. "Would you have my child, Lacey? Would you want my baby at your breast?"

The idea of Tyler's child nursing eagerly at her

breast, as Tyler was doing, brought a deep sense of joy to her. "Oh, yes, Ty. Oh, yes."

His lips left her breast and began to move leisurely toward her mouth. "Marry me, Lacey. I don't ever want this to end."

"Ty . . ."

"You don't have to answer right now. Just think about it."

He stepped inside the shower. Lacey wound her arms around his neck and held him tightly as the water cascaded over them. "I'll think about it, Ty," she whispered. He lifted her hips and joined their bodies again. They discovered to their delight that, even standing, they fit together very nicely.

It was after midnight before they finally ate strawberry and banana ice cream with chocolate syrup and cherries on top. It was almost dawn when they returned to Harmony Hall. They watched the sun come up from inside the newly refurbished gazebo, and when her father came down to start breakfast, he found them in the kitchen giggling as they attempted to feed each other sugary cereal and milk.

For the next few days everyone at Harmony Hall followed Tyler's directions for carrying out the renovations, while each day he drove into the city to work. Lacey happily ignored the fact that everybody knew they were in love. After the first few days Tyler didn't even bother to pretend to sleep in his studio or his apartment in town. Lacey was happier than she'd ever believed possible.

The weeks flew by, and the Craft House at Harmony Hall, as the venture had been dubbed, neared completion. Even Tyler had taken to spending long hours in this studio painting. Lacey wasn't allowed to see his work, and she didn't insist. It was enough that Tyler wanted to be there, to be a part of her life. He didn't really have to be an artist. Lacey loved him for making the attempt.

One Wednesday morning, as she sat in the living room making arrangements to move her supply of doll making materials from her mountain storage facility to her new studio in the barn, the telephone rang.

"Miss Lacey Lee Wilcox?" the crisp voice inquired.

"Yes, this is Lacey. If you're calling about leasing a stall in the Craft House, we have no more spaces available, and opening day is set for next Saturday."

"No, I'm afraid I don't know anything about the Craft House. My name is Ryan Gaither. I own GaiCo Toy Company, and I'd like to discuss a deal with you."

"What kind of deal?"

"We've seen your HuggieBaby dolls, and we'd like to make you an offer."

"I don't understand. What kind of an offer?"

"We'll buy your design and offer you a percentage of the retail sales. I'd like to arrange to meet with you in person and discuss the dollar amount."

Lacey was stunned. Finally she managed to say, "No, Mr. Gaither. I don't think so. You see, my HuggieBabies are very individual. They could never be mass-produced. I employ ladies who hand sew them. They'd be out of work. No, thank you, I'm not interested."

Tyler was in Atlanta, at his office. After she hung up, Lacey went out to the barn and walked down the middle corridor, watching the craftspeople putting the final touches on their booths. Tyler had arranged the shops so that each resident was provided with a tiny showroom in front, a workroom and sleeping quarters in the rear.

"Morning, Mr. Spragg. You've really accomplished a lot." The walls were covered with plaques ready to be carved with the names or initials of the buyers. Door emblems and wooden street signs were stacked against the wall.

"Yes, indeedy, Lacey. I'm a regular tycoon."

"How's the duck coming?"

Lacey caught a quick flash of longing on the little man's round face before he replaced it with a smile and answered. "Oh, I haven't worked on the duck for a while. Too busy getting ready for opening day. I'll get back to it—sometime."

The sound of someone playing musical scales on a piano tinkled from Arthur's studio. He had a growing number of pupils even before his work area was completed. For the last week Lacey hadn't heard one drum beat or flute solo from his bedroom. She'd never realized before how much she enjoyed having Arthur's whimsical music in the background. She even missed the African fertility music.

Lacey nodded at the new glassblower, the leather worker, and a slight young man who was arranging flowers in a studio he'd named The Silk Shop. Yes, Tyler had accomplished a lot. She could see where the Craft House would attract a sufficient number of people over the weekends to generate enough income for the artist to become self-supporting. Even her mother was working. After her parents had hired a secretary to organize their time, they'd made unbelievable progress. The only hint of discord came when her father decided against buying his polo pony, which disappointed her mother. He said he wouldn't have time to ride, now that his book was underway.

Lacey considered the offer that the GaiCo man had made. He'd finally, in desperation, named a dollar amount, and it was more money than she'd ever dreamed of. He seemed upset when she turned him down again.

The next day Lacey decided to pay the household accounts and went searching for the latest bills. In the top drawer of her mother's newly-organized desk, she found the mortgage notices. Shocked, her stomach in knots, she sat down and scanned them. She hadn't even know about a mortgage. The overdue notices from the first three months were polite. The collection letters that followed weren't. The last letter, dated six weeks ago, announced the pending foreclosure. The letterhead carried a company name in bold, dark letters. The officers' names were in smaller print. The officers were Win Maxwell and Tyler Winter.

Lacey felt as if her heart had contracted and shattered into a thousand painful pieces. Tyler hadn't come to Harmony Hall looking for her. He'd come to repossess her home, to turn it into an office park or a forest of condos. She stared at the evidence in stunned disbelief. The whole thing had been a lie. He'd lulled her parents into a false sense of security while he was plotting to take over the very home he'd been pretending to preserve. And he'd pretended to paint to keep himself close to the problem so he could head off any potential disasters.

Lacey dragged herself up to her room and flung

herself across the bed, the same bed where Tyler had made glorious love to her just the night before. Could she have been so wrong about him? She'd been totally convinced that he cared about her, about her crazy family. Would you have my babies? he'd asked. Even now her nipples felt drawn and sore from his sampling. There was a curious ripple in her lower body as it cried out for the touch of the man who had lied to her. What if she were already pregnant?

For over an hour she lay there, trying to make sense of what had happened. She couldn't have been mistaken; he'd wanted her. Maybe making her pregnant was part of the plan. He wouldn't have helped her family become self-sufficient unless he cared about her.

She thought about the problem for a long time until she finally determined his reasons. If her family could function without her, she could give up traveling to her craft shows and move into the city to be a proper wife to him. But what about Harmony Hall? In a few short weeks he'd taken over her role, arranging schedules and cajoling her parents and the other artists into motivating themselves even if they didn't want to.

Lacey thought back to Mr. Spragg's wistful dismissal of the completion of his duck. She remembered finding Spence's tap shoes in the trash. Had Arthur made any progress on writing his musical? Lacey had to know. The first thing she had to find out, however, was where Tyler's company stood on processing the foreclosure.

"So you're Lacey." Win Maxwell smiled and nodded his head as Lacey sat in the leather chair beside his desk. "All I've heard for the last six weeks is Lacey, Lacey, Lacey. You've really turned this office upside down."

"Then you know what's happened at Harmony Hall?"

"Oh, yes. I thought that Tyler had totally flipped out when he put his condo up for sale to pay off the mortgage, but when he began turning down invitations and cutting back on his working hours here, I knew it was the beginning of the end."

"He's paid off the mortgage?"

"Well, not technically—not yet. He's simply paid the past-due amount. Once the sale of the condo actually goes through, he'll retire the mortgage. I have to hand it to you, Lacey. I never thought I'd see Tyler Winter turn into a hippie."

"I don't understand, Mr. Maxwell. You're his partner. Why did you let him do it?"

"Me? Try to stop Tyler when he's made up his mind? I've never seen him so happy. And every move he's made has been for love. I can't help but wonder what will happen when all this planning and rebuilding is finished. Tyler's never been content to stay in one spot for long. I'll admit it, I hope he doesn't wake up to regret it one day."

"Don't let him pay the mortgage," Lacey said slowly as she rose from the chair. "I won't let him sacrifice his future for Harmony Hall, Mr. Maxwell, no matter what he thinks he wants. How much time do I have?"

"The condo is already on the market, and there's a buyer coming in on Monday to look it over. You don't have much time."

Monday. And today was Thursday. Tyler's business partner was right, she didn't have much time, she realized. But she couldn't let Tyler sell his condo and change his life-style. What if he discovered that he didn't like sharing the barn with her mother's artists? What if he woke up one day and saw the past few weeks as nothing more than temporary lunacy? She wouldn't be able to face the disappointment in his eyes.

He didn't belong in an artists' retreat. He'd tried the vagabond life once before, and he'd left it. As long as he still had his old way of life to go back to, he wouldn't feel threatened, and perhaps she could keep him in love with her. She had to take care of the mortgage and the expenses of Harmony Hall herself, just as she'd always done. And there was only one way she could do it.

Lacey stopped at a pay phone and made a call. She set up an appointment with Ryan Gaither of GaiCo Toys.

Nine

Tyler walked down the center corridor of the barn and smiled his approval. From the time he'd opened the gate that morning, there had been a steady stream of visitors to the grand opening of the Craft House at Harmony Hall. Even Alfred had gotten involved by acting as official host. Gynneth, resplendent in a flowing green hostess dress, was holding court in the garden, reciting poetry to the accompaniment of Arthur's lilting flute melodies.

Tyler searched for Lacey. She hadn't returned on Friday from her quick trip to her mountain warehouse, as she'd originally planned. She'd gotten back an hour ago, and he'd been so busy since the gate had opened, they'd barely had time to talk.

The visitors seemed pleased with the handmade crafts, and the artist's inventories were dwindling even more rapidly than he'd anticipated. Spence reported requests by several more artists for spots in the barn. Yes, his plan was working out, just as he'd envisioned. On Monday he'd sign the papers on the sale of his condo and pay off the mortgage on Harmony Hall. He'd give Lacey the deed as a wedding present. Married to Lacey, what a wonderful thought. He felt his chest swell with happiness.

"Lacey Lee," he murmured out loud, "where the heck are you?"

Tyler climbed to the barn's second story and began a systematic perusal of the grounds from the window. He caught sight of Lacey walking slowly past the pool into the woods beyond. There was something about the way she held her shoulders that gave her a defeated look. Something was wrong. Why hadn't he realized it before? She'd stayed away from him all morning. Tyler ran downstairs and headed after her. He passed the gazebo, where Gynneth was ending a recitation.

"Oh, Tyler?" she called out.

"Sorry, I'm on an urgent mission," he answered as he trotted past her through the crowd of visitors and into the cool, shadowy woods.

He found Lacey sobbing quietly, resting her head against the low limb of a massive tree.

"Darling, what's wrong?" Tyler wrapped his arms tightly around her. "Talk to me, Lacey."

"Oh, Tyler," she said in great despair. "Why didn't you tell me the truth?"

She turned around and gazed up at him with a tortured expression on her face. She knew about the mortgage, Tyler realized immediately. About the mortgage, and about the reason he had first come to Harmony Hall. "How did you find out?" he asked wearily.

"Find out? Didn't you think I'd find out?" She pulled herself out his arms and twisted away.

"Yes. No. I didn't know. I intended to tell you the first day. I did look for you for personal reasons, Lacey. I just didn't know that the Wilcoxes of Harmony Hall were your family. When I found out, I came right away. I didn't intend to keep the mortgage a secret, I swear. I just didn't want to lose you before I could figure out an answer."

The anguish in his voice was real, and Lacey understood, but she couldn't pretend that it hadn't happened. He'd deliberately taken over and made plans without being honest with her. Even now she couldn't be sure how he really felt about her. She knew he'd fallen in love with her family. Gynneth and Alfred were the mother and father he'd wished for and never had. What was she, just part of his fantasy?

"I understand, Tyler. I understand, but I can't let you do it. They're my relatives. I'll share them with you for as long as you need them, and me, but we don't expect you to pay for being here."

"Is that what you think, Lacey? That I'm paying for a place in your family?"

"I don't know, Tyler. I only know that I can't let you sell your home to pay off our mortgage. I can't let you drop out of your other life to become a part of mine. We don't fit together, Tyler, and you can't program yourself to belong here. I don't want you to have regrets."

"Lacey, look at me." Tyler turned her to face him, then placed his hand on her chin and lifted it gently. "You're wrong. We do fit together, in every way. Let me show you. I promise that you'll change your mind."

"No." She bit her lower lip, trying desperately to hold herself back from accepting his invitation, from the arms sliding around her waist. "Don't you see, Tyler? You can't take over people's lives and regiment them. What about Arthur's music? What about Mr. Spragg's duck? What about your real estate career?"

"I don't understand." Tyler's bewilderment was genuine.

"It doesn't matter," Lacey said in a low voice. "I do, and I've made arrangements to sell my Huggie-Babies to GaiCo Toy Company. They'll give me enough money to care for my family for the rest of their lives. They won't have to give up their whimsical little dreams in order to survive."

"Give up their dreams, darling? Don't you see, dreams are only blueprints. If they're meant to be followed, the dreamers will follow them. They just need a starting point. The Craft House is their starting point, Lacey. If Mr. Spragg wants to complete his duck, he will. If Arthur wants to write a Broadway musical score, he will. I've only kept their dreams from being killed by the demands of reality."

"But," Lacey argued, "you're giving up your dream to give us ours. I could never live with that."

"Perhaps in the beginning I didn't understand, my darling gypsy lady, but once I got involved with all of you I knew my old dream, my real dream, was still there, hidden beneath years of work and success, camouflaged by briefcases and business suits, dried out by beautiful women in cold, elegant bedrooms.

"Ah, Lacey, you can't give up your dolls, they're a part of you. I'll help you set up more efficient cost-accounting methods of production and better marketing techniques. We'll make HuggieBabies the next phenomenon of the toy world."

"I see, and while you're streamlining my home sewing production to work more efficiently, what will I be doing to earn your help?"

"Loving me?"

"You mean more sex, don't you?" Her voice started to break. "Is that our medium of exchange? I didn't realized my body was so valuable."

Tyler stiffened. His voice went painfully quiet. "Lacey Lee Wilcox, you're going to listen to me. You've been a martyr in looking after your family long enough. They can get along without you."

"They need me," she whispered desperately.

"They don't need you. You need them. It's time you stopped hiding behind their needs to keep yourself from failure. You don't want to reach out for love. Your family gives you an excuse not to. If you think that selling your dolls to support your family is the answer, you're kidding yourself. Your mother just wants you to have what she's shared with your father. Even your sister reached out for love. And Arthur's day will come. Then where will you be? How in hell are you going to find answers to your needs once your family is happy without your help?"

"I'll survive," she managed in a tight voice. "I don't need anybody."

"Not even me?"

She looked at him with tormented eyes. Years of bitterness and self-denial overflowed inside her and she lashed out at him before she could stop to examine the reason. "Not even you, Tyler."

The blood drained out of his face, and she knew she'd hurt him deeply.

"Fine. I'm gone. I'll clean out my studio later," he said in a low, dead voice. Then he turned and walked away without looking back.

Lacey leaned against the tree, her body drained of strength and her mind churning with confusion. She stood in silent despair, watching Tyler disappear beyond the trees before she sought refuge in her turret bedroom.

The crowds began to filter away as the afternoon faded into night. It was nearly nine o'clock when a light knock sounded on her door.

"Lace? Are you in there? Everybody's gone."

It was Arthur. He knocked again. "Go away. I'm tired." She couldn't face her family tonight. For nearly three hours she'd gone over and over the ugly scene in her mind.

"No way, sis. We need to talk."

"All right," she finally agreed, "come in."

"I heard what happened this afternoon. I was on my way into the woods to meditate. That was dumb, Lace," Arthur's voice cut through the silence. "You finally find a man who wants to love you, and you won't let him do it." Lacey straightened hurriedly as Arthur stepped into her bedroom and sat down on the bed.

"You listened?"

"Sorry," he muttered. "I didn't mean to eavesdrop." He came to her and touched her shoulder. "You're giving up a terrific guy, Lace."

"What do you know about it?" Lacey cried. "All he wants to do is . . . organize everything and run my life. Your life. Mother's and Father's."

"And which part are you objecting to?"

"All of it." She leaned against Arthur and sobbed into his shoulder. "I love him, and I don't know what to do about it. I can't let him give up everything for us."

"But you'd give up everything for him, wouldn't you?"

"Not for him," she began, then stopped short. Arthur was right. If she sold HuggieBabies, it would be to protect Tyler as much as it would be to protect her family. She loved him too much to let him give up everything for her. "You're right, Arthur, it would be for him."

"Sounds to me like two people in love. I wouldn't take a chance on losing that, Lacey. If I were you, I'd go to him and talk."

Her brother put his arm around her, and she leaned gratefully against him.

"Oh, Arthur, what if you're right?" Was her foolish attempt at emotional independence costing her the man she loved. Lacey didn't know. She only knew that she had never been so unhappy in her life.

"I'm right, Lacey. Trust me."

"I have to think about it, Arthur. I'm not sure I can change enough for him. He wants me to stop looking after Mother and Father."

"And I'm sure that they'll be grateful to Tyler if you do."

"What do you mean, Arthur? What in hell will Mother and Daddy do without me?"

"Why don't you ask them? I think their answer might surprise you. What I'm more interested to know is what you're going to do without Tyler."

"You're serious, aren't you?" Lacey stared at her mother in disbelief.

"Please, darling. We've loved having you feel responsible for us, and we haven't wanted to appear ungrateful, but you're so efficient."

"Now, Gynneth," Alfred Wilcox interrupted, "don't be too hard on her. We knew what she was doing all along. We could have insisted that she stop hiding behind our needs. We let her take charge because she needed to. And then it got to be easier and easier for us, and eventually we stopped trying."

"I never realized you felt that way," Lacey said slowly.

"We didn't realize it either, until Tyler came along and turned back the clock. Don't you see Lacey? Harmony Hall is going to be what we'd wanted it to be all along, and we'll have done it ourselves."

"Well, maybe," Lacey said under her breath, "and maybe this will be my last efficient move as a Wilcox." Once the mortgage was paid they wouldn't be obligated to Tyler, or anybody else. They'd never know what it cost her to do it.

Arthur had been right on all counts. She couldn't imagine life without Tyler. Harmony Hall and her own stubborn pride had cost her the man she loved, and she didn't know how to get along without him. She'd been hiding behind her family because she'd been afraid to reach out for love.

At sunup the next morning Lacey was still pacing the floor. As the hours passed she'd become more and more morose over her foolish treatment of Tyler. So he had wanted to repossess Harmony Hall. He hadn't done it, and several times he had tried to tell her something and she didn't let him. Had she been wrong in her evaluation of Tyler Winter?

From her spot up high, Lacey watched for Tyler's red truck, but it never came. Finally she made up her mind. She wasn't proud. By gum and by golly she'd been wrong, and it was up to her to right the error. She showered and changed her clothes, dressing carefully in a white eyelet sundress and white leather sandals. She pinned a sprig of white wildflowers in her hair and left her room with great resolve. She drove the lavender van straight into the parking lot of Tyler's office building and marched into his office.

Tyler wasn't there. He wasn't at home either. He wouldn't answer his phone or his door. Win Maxwell hadn't heard a word from his partner. The only person she did reach was Ryan Gaither at GaiCo Toys. She told him that she'd changed her mind, Lacey's HuggieBabies weren't for sale.

With a heavy heart Lacey drove her van back to Harmony Hall and parked it. She avoided her family and the artists in residence and headed back to her tower bedroom. She wouldn't cry. She'd get mad. Sooner or later she'd find Tyler Winter and she'd torture him. She'd string him up on the nearest tree and stick hat pins under his toenails, and then she'd . . .

And then she saw the red pickup truck as it turned into the space by the barn. Tyler! He'd come back. She'd apologize for acting like a child. Lacey wiped her face and broke into a run. By the time she reached the barn, she was smiling. By the time she swept into his bedroom studio, locked the door, and pulled the stern-faced man with a day-old beard into her arms, she was picking out names for the baby she hoped they'd have.

"I love you, Tyler. I'm going to have trouble accepting this change of heart you've had about your life-style, but I'm not going to chase you away

because of it. I'm going to build a balcony around
your bed and chain you to it. I'm going to keep
you barefoot and exhausted until I'm pregnant.
Any help you give me with my HuggieBabies is
going to result in producing the real kind."

"Lacey . . . why . . . what . . ."

"I know, I know, forget what I said yesterday. I
was confused. No, hellfire and damnation, I wasn't
confused, I was dead wrong. And I'm not selling
my dolls, so you'd better be sure about moving in
here."

"Are *you* sure, Lacey? That's the important
question."

"I'm still confused about some things. But not
about you and me."

He smiled slowly, letting the hurt slide away
until his face was filled with quiet joy. "Do you
want a chain right now?"

She was already nude, and Tyler's clothes were
falling to the floor as quickly as Lacey could un-
button and unzip them. "For what?"

"To tie me to the bed. I love you, Lacey Lee
Wilcox, you crazy lady. And I'll stay right here as
long as it takes to prove it. I've already sold my
condo, but I haven't paid off the mortgage. We'll
do that together, eventually—all of us—when we've
made enough money on our crafts."

"Can we?"

"If what Spence tells me it true, we won't have
any trouble. Now, what about that chain? You've
already taken over my heart and mind. My body is
begging to be next."

They settled down on the foam rubber pallet he
was using for a bed, and she held him fiercely,
her tears falling on his chest like warm rain. "Oh,
Tyler, are you sure that you love me?"

Tyler's heart was pounding. His body was already ready to comply with every request she made. But he wanted to say the words she needed to hear too. No more secrets, no more half-truths.

"Sure? Lacey, I'm crazy about you. I love your family, but only because they're a part of you." His hand slid between her legs, encouraging her, demanding and receiving a breathless response. His voice dropped to a low rasp. "I have something I have to show you. But first—"

"Show me, Tyler," Lacey said, nibbling his chin, rubbing her fingertips wildly across his chest, clasping his body to hers with an urgency that she couldn't hide. And he did. Afterwards, as she lay quiet in his arms, he kissed her lips, then moved downward and kissed her stomach, then reclaimed her lips with such ardor that Lacey knew she'd never need a rope or a chain to keep his attention from wandering. He stood up and pulled on his pants.

"Tyler? No. Why . . ."

"Ssssh. You'll see." When he had his pants on, he started across the room and paused at the open window, a grin on his face. He leaned his head out the window and yelled, "Yahoo! I'm getting married!" to a startled Spence, who was crossing the parking area below. Spence greeted the announcement with a thumbs up sign. "And we're going to have a baby—soon!" Mr. Spraggs joined Spence and they began to applaud.

Back at the bed, he took Lacey's hand and gently pulled her to her feet.

"Don't you think you're a little crazy?" she asked, nearly bursting with pride. "I'm probably not even pregnant yet."

"Definitely crazy—crazy and happy. If you're not, we'll just have to work at it. And I'm a very hard worker. Ah, Lacey, I lay night after night praying that I'd given you a baby. I was afraid it was the only way I'd get you to admit we belonged together."

He seemed unable to stop touching her, and Lacey wouldn't have it any other way, but when he took her nipple in his mouth, she winced.

"What's wrong?" He pulled back, instantly concerned.

"They're just a little tender," she admitted, "but don't stop. If I'm going to nurse our child, I have to be tough."

"Our child." He rested his hand on her stomach. "I think I must have known we'd be together from the moment you jumped over that banister and landed on top of me. Even then I was falling in love with you. Now I'll show you what you've given me."

He turned Lacey to face the canvas he had covered with a cloth in one corner of the room. He went to it, anxiously removed the cover, and stood back, waiting for her reaction.

Lacey felt her heart contract. All her doubts vanished. He'd been telling the truth. Tyler was an artist, a real artist, maybe the only true artist in her mother's retreat.

The picture was a soft, muted swirl of blue, pale peach, and soft yellow depicting a woman. The woman was sitting on a balcony rail, her body nude in the late afternoon sunshine. At her breast was a child, suckling in contentment. The woman was gazing past the child at the artist with a look of such intense love that Lacey's eyes filled with tears, and she couldn't speak. The woman was a serene Madonna, the personification of sensual love, a statement of the heart so overwhelming, no one could fail to notice that the portrait was painted with devotion in every stroke.

Tyler had painted what he was afraid to ask for, her deepest commitment and the child he'd wanted her to give him.

"And now you know," Tyler whispered hesitantly. "You've made me love again, and in loving you, I've found a part of me that I'd turned away from. Selling my condo and cutting back on my business is what I have to do, because I've found something much more important to me."

Tears slipped down Lacey's face. "Tyler . . . Ty . . . it's beautiful. I'm so ashamed. I truly didn't know you were such a talented artist. Is that the way you see me?"

"That's the way you are, darling. Giving, loving, and made to be loved."

He walked back to the bed and pulled her down beside him. Lacey took his hand and kissed it, first the palm, then each finger. "So much talent," she whispered. "So much love." They sat silent for nearly a minute, touching each other and looking at the painting. Noise from the shops downstairs began to filter into their reverie. Lacey put an anxious hand over her mouth. "Ty, do you think that everyone heard us making love?"

He smiled coyly. "I think I'm glad your studio is beneath mine. At least it's vacant. Maybe we can build a connecting door through the ceiling."

From Arthur's studio came the unmistakable strains of a flute playing "Rock A Bye Baby." Lacey gasped and began to giggle. Tyler leaned down grinning, and whispered, "I guess we weren't as discrete as we'd hoped."

"Maybe," Lacey quipped. "Maybe we ought to send down a request for something a bit more lively—bagpipes, cymbals, a thirty-two piece orchestra—at least for a little while." She turned back to Tyler. She'd give him her body—and her dreams.

"One thing," Tyler said dryly. "We won't have to spend much money on shoes."

"I hope not," Lacey agreed, and opened her lips for his kiss. "As long as I have you and my place here, I'm going to love being barefoot."

So am I, thought Tyler as he sealed their futures with a kiss. He and Lacey would attend another wedding together, but this time he'd be the groom and she'd be the bride. He'd place his ring on her finger and claim her for all time.

There was a sudden upswing in the tempo of the music below, and Tyler could swear that the melody was a variation of the wedding march. The morning sun moved across the sky, and Lacey slept. Tyler lay awake, holding her tenderly. Nothing he had ever accomplished in his life seemed as important as keeping her happy and beside him. Every good thing he did for the rest of his life would be for love of Lacey.

THE EDITOR'S CORNER

We sail into our LOVESWEPT summer with six couples who, at first glance, seem to be unlikely matches. What they all have in common, and the reason that everything works out in the end, is Cupid's arrow. When true love strikes, there's no turning back—not for Shawna and Parker, her fiance, who doesn't even remember that he's engaged; not for Annabella and Terry, who live in completely different worlds; not for Summer and Cabe, who can't forget their teenage love. Holly and Steven were never meant to fall in love—Holly was supposed to get a juicy story, not a marriage proposal, from the famous bachelor. And our last two couples for the month are probably the most unlikely matches of all—strangers thrown together for a night who can't resist Cupid's arrow and turn an evening of romance into a lifetime of love!

We're very pleased to introduce Susan Crose to you this month. With **THE BRASS RING,** she's making her debut as a LOVESWEPT author—and what a sparkling debut it is! Be on the lookout for the beautiful cover on this book—it's our first bride and groom in a long time!

THE BRASS RING, LOVESWEPT #264, opens on the eve of Shawna McGuire's and Parker Harrison's wedding day when it seems that nothing can mar their perfect joy and anticipation on becoming husband and wife. But there's a terrible accident, and Shawna is left waiting at the church. Shawna almost loses her man, but she never gives up, and finally they do get to say their vows. This is a story about falling in love with the same person twice, and what could be more romantic than that?

Joan Elliott Pickart's **THE ENCHANTING MISS ANNA-BELLA,** LOVESWEPT #265, is such an enchanting love story that I guarantee you won't want to put this book down. Miss Annabella is the librarian in Harmony, Oklahoma, and Terry Russell is a gorgeous, blue-eyed, ladykiller pilot who has returned to the tiny town to visit his folks. All the ladies in Harmony fantasize about handsome Terry Russell, but Annabella doesn't even know what a fantasy is! Annabella's a late bloomer, and Terry is the

(continued)

one who helps her to blossom. Terry sees the woman hidden inside, and he falls in love with her. Annabella discovers herself, and then she can return Terry's love. When that happens, it's a match made in heaven!

FLYNN'S FATE, by Patt Bucheister, LOVESWEPT #266, is another example of this author's skill in touching our emotions. Summer Roberts loves the small town life and doesn't trust Cabe Flynn, the city slicker who lives life in Chicago's fast lane. Cabe was her teenage heartthrob, but years ago he gave up on Clearview and on Summer. Now he's back to claim his legacy, and Summer finds she can't bear to spend time with him because he awakens a sweet, wild hunger in her. Cabe wants to explore the intense attraction between them; he won't ignore his growing desire. He knows his own mind, and he also knows that Summer is his destiny—and with moonlight sails and words of love, he shows her this truth.

In **MADE FOR EACH OTHER** by Doris Parmett, LOVE-SWEPT #267, it's our heroine Holly Anderson's job to get an exclusive interview from LA's most eligible bachelor. Steven Chadwick guards his privacy so Holly goes undercover to get the scoop. She has no problem getting to know the gorgeous millionaire—in fact, he becomes her best friend and constant companion. Steven is too wonderful for words, and too gorgeous to resist, and Holly knows she must come clean and risk ruining their relationship. When friendly hugs turn into sizzling embraces, Holly gives up her story to gain his love. Best friends become best lovers! Doris Parmett is able to juggle all the elements of this story and deliver a wonderfully entertaining read.

STRICTLY BUSINESS by Linda Cajio, LOVESWEPT #268, maybe should have been titled, "Strictly Monkey Business". That describes the opening scene where Jess Brannen and Nick Mikaris wake up in bed together, scarcely having set eyes on each other before! They are both victims of a practical joke.

Things go from bad to worse when Jess shows up for a job interview and finds Nick behind the desk. They can't seem to stay away from each other, and Nick can't

(continued)

forget his image of her in that satin slip! Jess keeps insisting that she won't mix business with pleasure, even when she has the pleasure of experiencing his wildfire kisses. She doth protest too much—and finally her "no" becomes a "yes." This is Linda Cajio's sixth book for LOVESWEPT, and I know I speak for all your fans when I say, "Keep these wonderful stories coming, Linda!"

One of your favorite LOVESWEPT authors, Helen Mittermeyer, has a new book this month, and it's provocatively—and appropriately!—titled **ABLAZE**, LOVESWEPT #269. Heller Blane is a stunning blond actress working double shifts because she's desperately in need of funds. But is she desperate enough to accept $10,000 from a mysterious stranger *just* to have dinner with him? Conrad Wendell is dangerously appealing, and Heller is drawn to him. When their passionate night is over, she makes her escape, but Conrad cannot forget her. He's fallen in love with his vanished siren—she touched his soul—and he won't be happy until she's in his arms again. Thank you, Helen, for a new LOVESWEPT. **ABLAZE** has set our hearts on fire!

The HOMETOWN HUNK CONTEST is coming! We promised you entry blanks this month, but due to scheduling changes, the contest will officially begin next month. Just keep your eyes open for the magnificent men in your own hometown, then learn how to enter our HOMETOWN HUNK CONTEST *next month*.

Happy reading!

Sincerely,

Carolyn Nichols

Carolyn Nichols
 Editor
LOVESWEPT
Bantam Books
666 Fifth Avenue
New York, NY 10103

THE DELANEY DYNASTY

Men and women whose loves and passions are so glorious it takes many great romance novels by three bestselling authors to tell their tempestuous stories.

THE SHAMROCK TRINITY

THE DELANEYS OF KILLAROO

THE DELANEYS: *The Untamed Years*

Buy these books at your local bookstore or use the handy coupon below.
